THE SIGNATURE

DI GILES BOOK 19

ANNA-MARIE MORGAN

ALSO BY ANNA-MARIE MORGAN

For my Family

PROLOGUE

Her breath came in short, laboured bursts as the cold air stung her face and pained her lungs. She would have given up, but this was no ordinary run. It was life or death; the girl forced her limbs onward.

Numbing cold gave way to heat as the chill penetrated deep into her skin, misleading the pain receptors lying within. She tossed her bag and jacket to the ground.

The monster was coming. A vile beast, hard on her heels, grunting and panting. So much noise.

He had followed her from the car, pounding the earth somewhere behind. Somewhere she dared not look.

As she tumbled into the frozen dirt, grit and stone scraped and penetrated the numbed the skin on her knees, hands, and cheek.

Still it came: the thump, thump, thump of feet. Bang, bang, bang in her ears as she lay on the ground panting for air.

The girl dragged herself up and sprinted on towards the light coming from a barn. At last, somewhere to hide.

She ripped off her blouse, tossing that too before reaching the shed door, heaving it open, and crouching inside.

Gradually her breathing slowed as an overwhelming urge to sleep replaced the fear.

Let the monster come. She no longer cared.

1

A THIEF IN THE NIGHT

She flicked a glance behind, breath catching in her throat; heels snagging on uneven paving stones. Only cold stone buildings and parked cars inhabited the surrounding space. She pressed a hand to her chest to calm her thudding heart, chiding herself for being so foolish. Imagination could create many monsters, given free rein. Her breath, clouding in the frozen night air, amplified the eerie feeling she was not alone.

The young woman rounded the corner. A half-hour walk across town and she would be home, changing into cotton pyjamas, brushing her teeth, and going to bed with a warm drink and a good book. A hot chocolate might weaken the hangover that must surely come with morning light.

Somewhere overhead, a lamp flickered. Its beam sent juddering shadows creeping over the walls. The girl pulled her long coat tighter, stumbling and cursing as the hard leather of new shoes blistered her heels. "This is silly," she whispered. "Pull yourself together. There is nothing to be afraid of."

As she approached a derelict church and a closed chip

shop, a large gloved hand reeking of stale sweat and leather clamped over her mouth, while a powerful arm like a fire-fighter's hydraulic jaws wrapped around her waist, dragging her through an alleyway and behind the disused church. Her feet bumped over clumps of weeds and broken bottles as she struggled with her attacker, eventually stamping hard as she could on his instep. Her kitten heels made little impression on steel-toe-capped boots. He was too strong.

"Shut up and listen," he hissed. "If you do as I say, you won't get hurt. Continue to struggle and I will kill you."

Her muffled screams were not enough to waken the neighbours. Not a single window lit up. No curtains twitched. No doors opened.

He replaced the gloved hand with a wet cloth that smelled overwhelmingly like nail polish remover, and her legs lost their strength.

In her staring eyes, the street lights faded away.

"ONE COFFEE WITH MILK, and no sugar." Dewi handed her a white mug with 'Meh!' printed on the side.

"Thank you. That should help clear my head." She gave her DS a weak smile while reading the inscription. It echoed how she felt that morning: meh, with a thick head that hadn't quite developed into a full-blown headache. If it had, she could have taken a painkiller. Instead, a woolly brain exacerbated her Monday morning blues.

These mild headaches had occurred regularly over the last several weeks, and her once regular periods were now erratic and waning. Perhaps, she mused, this was the onset of the change of life, the hormonal upheaval a woman must suffer at around her age.

"I thought I'd bring you up to speed." Dewi unbuttoned his suit jacket, pushing both hands into his trouser pockets.

"With what?" She sipped the hot liquid, comforted by its warmth, her hands still cold from the drive in to work because she had forgotten her gloves that morning.

"A young woman, Jacky Bevan, nineteen years old, went missing Saturday night from town. She was expected home from a night out with her friends, but didn't return. Her parents are frantic, and insisting that this is highly unusual behaviour. It isn't our case, not yet. Uniform are taking the lead. She may have spent the night with someone but, if so, it wasn't with any of her friends. They are worried about her. If she doesn't turn up in the next twenty-four hours, we ought to look into it."

"Agreed." Yvonne nodded. "Where was she drinking? Do they have CCTV?"

"They're collecting and reviewing all the footage they can. Her last drinks were at the Cambrian Vaults on the corner of New Road and Short Bridge Street. I've asked the sergeant downstairs to keep me informed of progress."

"What was her intention when she left the Cambrian Vaults? Was she getting a taxi or walking home? Was she with someone else? Did she get a lift?"

"They won't know for sure until they have reviewed the footage, but they believe she walked. Her mum received a text from Jacky just before midnight to say she intended leaving the pub shortly after. She didn't say how she was getting home, but she wasn't afraid of walking alone, and had done so many times in the past, apparently."

"I see... I am surprised her friends didn't put her in a taxi or check that she got home safely."

"They wanted to call her a cab, but claim she insisted on walking."

"Had there been trouble? An argument?"

Dewi shrugged. "I only know what I have told you, I'm afraid."

"Where was she headed?"

"She lives with her mum, dad, and brother on the Trehafren Estate."

"Isn't that the other end of town?"

"Yes, it's on the Llanidloes Road, approximately one mile from the Cambrian. She would have set off along New Road, and on from there."

"That's a fair distance for a young woman at night, under the influence of alcohol."

"Yes, but it's the main road through the town, and well lit. Perhaps she felt safe enough?"

"Let's hope she went with someone she knew, and that she gets in touch with family and friends today. Keep me informed please, Dewi."

"Will do, ma'am." He left the DI alone with her thoughts and the rest of her rapidly cooling tea.

She turned her gaze to the window, pursing her lips. Hoar frost clung to the branches of the trees outside. The temperature had dropped to minus seven during the night. Not the sort of weather you could be out in for long, especially if not dressed for it.

2

LIKE SO MUCH RUBBISH

When she entered the station on Tuesday morning, Yvonne was swamped by a team of uniformed officers, running past while donning helmets, stab vests, and ear pieces as they headed for vans in the car park. While still receiving instructions from the operator on their radios, they speed away, lights and sirens blaring.

"What's going on?" She asked Callum as he rushed down the stairs, cigarette tucked behind one ear.

"Jacky Bevan, the missing nineteen-year-old, has been found. Did you not get my message?" He frowned.

"No, I didn't." She pulled her mobile from her jacket pocket. "Damn, I put it on silent while I was at the GP surgery last night. I forgot to switch it back to noisy." She eyed the five missed calls and text message notifications. "I'm sorry, Callum."

"No problem... She was found in rubbish bins in the carpark at the back of the fish bar, along from the Cambrian Vaults."

"Oh, hell... Foul play?"

"Don't know yet. Everybody is heading down there. Dewi is on his way." He threw on an overcoat, pulling the cigarette from behind his ear.

"Okay," she answered. "You go ahead. I'll wait for Dewi and catch you up."

Callum nodded before continuing down the stairs, two at a time.

NEW ROAD WAS awash with activity. Inside lines of police tape, several incident vehicles and ambulances had parked along the road next to the fish bar, and groups of onlookers stood shivering beyond the cordon at both ends.

Yvonne and Dewi flashed their badges at a uniformed officer standing guard at the entrance to the carpark at the back of the chip shop.

He nodded, waving them through.

Hazmat-suited SOCO officers photographed the girl as she lay in the bottle-green dumpster, before carefully documenting and extracting the rubbish found with her.

Pathologist Roger Hanson waited at the bin as the body was levered onto a stretcher.

The DI approached him. "What are we looking at? Was she murdered?"

He pursed his lips. "Hard to say, really. There are no obvious signs of foul play but, until I have a closer look, it's not clear how she died. Saturday was freezing, and we know she had been drinking. Perhaps she climbed in to keep warm, but succumbed to hypothermia. She is curled into the foetal position, which may have been an attempt to keep warm."

The DI pursed her lips. "I hear what you are saying, and I know guys sometimes climb into dumpsters on frosty nights to sleep off intoxication, but a young woman? That would be highly unusual."

Hanson scratched his head. "Did her friends say how drunk she was?"

"I haven't had the chance to speak with them. Until now, it was considered a simple missing person's case. They thought she might have stayed at someone's house for the night. I'll know a lot more after the briefing this afternoon."

"And I'll know the cause of death after the autopsy." Hanson grimaced. "Not a nice place to end your life."

"It isn't." The DI shuddered. "I hope she didn't suffer."

Hanson headed over to the SOCO officers, leaving Yvonne to ponder the girl's death alone.

"She'd been in there at least twelve hours." Dewi rejoined her. "There were two rubbish bags on top of Jacky's body, put there yesterday evening by staff from the fish bar."

"And they didn't see her inside the bin?"

"They said they didn't look. They just opened the lid and tossed in the bags. People rarely peer inside when they put the rubbish out. It was only when the chip shop owner, Frances Howells, checked the levels in the bin that the girl was discovered. Frances says she inspects the dumpsters periodically because the smell is bad for business when they are overflowing."

"I see. How long had it been since she last checked them?"

"She says she looked in them Friday night, but didn't check them over the weekend."

"I see..." Yvonne turned her gaze to the covered stretcher being loaded into a private ambulance. "Poor girl..."

"There was something unusual amongst the rubbish." Dewi frowned.

"What do you mean?"

"A lidded jar was left on top of one of the rubbish bags near the girl's feet. Inside there was the brown skin of an onion, and a used match. Someone had removed the label from the jar."

The DI tilted her head. "Have forensics got it?"

He nodded. "They are taking everything from the bin for examination, in case the girl was murdered."

"Good... Something is off. I am not buying that a young woman would come down here late at night to sleep in a bin. It's poorly lit; there's a high fence surrounding the carpark; you have unlit garages at the back, and a derelict church with smashed windows. At night, this would give me the heebie-jeebies. I think most women would feel uncomfortable coming down here after dark even if they hadn't been drinking. And how would she know those bins were here?"

Dewi scratched his stubble. "Well, it is behind a fish restaurant; chances are there would be substantial-sized bins behind an eatery."

"I hope I am wrong, but I suspect someone else was involved in whatever happened to that girl." She peered up at the CCTV camera near the flat roof of the chip shop. It pointed directly at the parking area at the back of the establishment. "Was that camera working? Make sure we have a copy of any footage they have from Saturday evening onwards. I think it would have an excellent view of those bins."

"Will do. The camera belongs to probation. I'll make sure we get whatever feed they have."

As she cast her eyes over the rear of the fish restaurant, a young man appeared in the open doorway. Dressed in jeans and a white t-shirt, he hand-combed brown hair out of his eyes as his gaze darted this way and that, taking in the activity around the car park. He finally realised Yvonne was watching him and pushed his hands into his pockets.

She couldn't read his thoughts. His rugged face had no expression. She stepped forward, about to ask him who he was, but a woman called out and he ducked back, closing the door.

"That is Frances Howell's twenty-four-year-old son Tony." Dewi informed her. "I spoke to him when we arrived. He's taken the day off work to support his mother. She's in shock, and wanted him here. He arrived just before we did, apparently."

"I see." She turned her gaze back to the bin. "We'll need statements from them both."

"On it." Dewi nodded. "I've taken a few notes already, and they have agreed to give formal statements to uniform this afternoon. We'll get copies shortly after."

"Good." She turned back towards their vehicle. "We should set up an incident room. I have a feeling this death was murder."

YVONNE SURVEYED the faces in a room filled with uniformed and CID officers. Some sat with pen and notepads at the ready. Others yawned and nattered to each other.

She cleared her throat. "Thank you all for coming. I will keep this brief."

The chatter died down.

"As you will all be aware, missing nineteen-year-old Jacky Bevan was found deceased in a rubbish bin this morning. I'm told there were no immediate signs of foul play, but we should have the results of the autopsy later, and toxicology results will follow. If Jacky climbed into that bin of her own accord, then obviously we will not be pursuing a criminal investigation. I have called you all together, however, because I find it hard to believe she entered that bin of her own volition."

Someone coughed in the middle row.

"Believe me, I am not trying to make extra work for anyone, but there was no precedent. Miss Bevan had never stayed out at night before and had walked home after evenings out on several previous occasions. So, I urge you to speak to her friends and contacts, and to knock on doors in the immediate area on New Road. Does anyone know anything? Did anyone see anything? I will speak with her family later. They do not believe she would have climbed into a rubbish bin for warmth either, and are unhappy about a local radio station suggesting she got into it voluntarily. I am asking my team to delve into her social media for anything that could be relevant." She smoothed down her black cotton skirt. "We know she met up with friends for Christmas holiday drinks. What do they know? Did she say anything to them? Did any of them accompany her out of the pub or watch her leave the premises? Was someone lurking outside? Go through every scrap of footage from CCTV in the area and speak to residents who might have witnessed something from their windows."

The DI turned her gaze to the interactive whiteboard, where the dead girl's vivid blue eyes smiled from an enlarged photograph. Her face, peppered with freckles, was framed by shoulder-length red hair. "If Jacky climbed into that bin on her own, the only thing we will have lost is a little of our time. If she was put there by someone else, we will have a head start in finding out who was responsible, and why. Any questions?"

DC Dai Clayton leaned back in his chair. "Unfortunately, there are few residential properties in the immediate area, and the businesses and dental surgeries nearby are obviously closed at night. Even the fish bar is shuttered by midnight."

The DI nodded. "That is why the CCTV footage will be critical."

Dai cleared his throat. "And I have bad news on that front, I'm afraid."

Yvonne frowned. "Meaning?"

"Two street cameras had the potential to pick up Jacky as she left the Cambrian and walked along New Road towards the fish bar."

"Go on..."

"Both of them were out."

A murmur travelled through the room.

"What do you mean, out? Are you telling me they were not working?"

"Yes."

"Why? Were they undergoing scheduled maintenance?"

"No." Dai ran a hand through his mussed mop of brown hair. "I've spoken to engineers, and they are at a loss to explain the missing footage. The cameras stopped working at ten-thirty pm on Friday night. They said they are working on the problem and should have them up and running again soon. The whole of that part of the street was out, I'm afraid."

"What about Probation? Have we got their footage for the weekend?"

"We have," Dai replied. "But their camera was hampered by a high-sided transit van, whose owner we are still trying to locate. It was parked directly in front of those bins. We have the vehicle reg, and it is owned by one Peter Turner, who lives on Kerry Road."

"We should speak to him. Where is the van at the moment?"

"We haven't located it yet. I'll ask him to come in when we find out where he is. His neighbour told me he drives for a living, so it's not unusual for him to be away a few days at a time."

"Good work, Dai. Thank you for getting on with all of that."

Dai rubbed his cheek, shifting in his chair. "No problem... Callum helped."

"Well, thank you, both. We should have a more accurate time of death after the autopsy. The only concrete times we have at the moment are when she left the Cambrian on Friday night, and when the fifty-year-old chip shop owner, Frances Howells, discovered the body on Monday morning. Let's do everything we can to find out what happened in the intervening time."

The scraping of chairs and the rise of chatter accompanied the end of the briefing.

Yvonne studied the whiteboard and the meagre details they had so far, updating it with the information from Dai.

"It isn't much, is it?" Dewi stood at her shoulder.

"Perhaps Peter Turner can add something?" She pursed her lips. "Why was he parked in the chip shop car park when he lives on Kerry Road?"

"The most likely reason is the lack of parking outside his house."

"We should speak with Frances Howells again and find out whether Turner was in the habit of parking his vehicle there. If he wasn't, and Jacky's death was a murder, we may have our first suspect."

"Right-oh."

"And I think Callum and Dai ought to go through relevant social media. Let's find out what was going on in Jacky's life prior to her death."

THE PATHOLOGIST ROGER HANSON was deep in conversation with his assistant, both of them in scrubs, ready to begin the autopsy on Jacqueline Bevan.

He turned to greet the DI as she arrived. "Ah, Yvonne, just in time..."

"Thanks." She grimaced. "I was stuck in traffic." She took off her coat, hanging it on a peg with her bag before approaching the table where the girl lay cold, still and drained of colour. Her face was peaceful, however, as though she was merely sleeping. "Do you still think it was a natural death?"

"So far..." Hanson nodded. "I think she was dead within twelve hours of leaving the pub. There was no remaining rigor mortis when she was found, and no evidence of her body having been moved. Lividity was consistent with the foetal position in which she was found. She was fully clothed, aside from her jacket, which she or someone else had removed. It was found in the dumpster with her."

"Could she have climbed into that bin herself?"

"Yes. She has some mild bruising and scrapes to her skin, which would be consistent with a climb and subsequent fall into the bin. We have taken swabs from various locations on the body and are awaiting results, but I can see no outward sign of sexual assault. There are no wounds to the body that resulted in bleeding."

"I see."

Hanson made his Y-shaped incision before examining, extracting, and weighing organs.

The DI looked away occasionally as the assistant noted down Hanson's observations.

"The organ weights are within the normal range and are unremarkable. The hyoid bone is intact," he said to Yvonne, eventually. "I can't be certain until we have the bloods and toxicology results back, but what I am seeing is consistent with a death by hypothermia after climbing into that bin. Her clothing was inadequate for the temperatures that night. I think she removed her coat because she felt hot. That would be entirely consistent with dying from exposure. Though I should tell you, death from hypothermia is difficult to diagnose after someone has been drinking alcohol. Ethanol prevents some of the histochemical changes associated with that type of death. However, there was haemorrhaging in muscle tissue which would support the diagnosis of hypothermic death."

"Could she have been forced into that bin while someone held the lid down?"

"I can't rule that out." Hanson peeled off his gloves before pushing his glasses up onto his head. "But there is no damage to her hands, meaning she didn't try bashing her way out. I suspect she died after falling asleep."

"I see." The DI nodded. "When are you expecting the blood and toxicology results?"

"I am hoping to get them sometime tomorrow afternoon."

"Okay, can you send me through a copy as soon as you have them, along with your thoughts?"

"Absolutely." He nodded. "I'll phone you after I have emailed the report. If you have questions, you can fire them at me then."

"Great, thank you." She nodded to his assistant. "I'll leave you two to get on."

3

UNPALATABLE CONCLUSIONS

Yvonne and Dewi parked their car at the back of a three-bedroomed terraced house in Trehafren.

The red brick and white cladding facade was typical of houses on the estate. The homes had been built for factory workers in the seventies, when the Welsh Development Board aimed to attract people to the area following the decline of the woollen industry in Wales.

It was now a thriving estate, surrounded by rolling hills and bounded on one side by the River Severn. It was blessed with ample parking for residents and visitors alike, which came in handy when they needed to pay someone a visit.

They accessed the front of the house via a narrow alley. Dewi rang the bell on the PVC double-glazed door.

It was answered by a thin-faced, red-haired young man with dark rings under his eyes, and a few meagre whiskers worth of beard on his chin.

Yvonne flashed her badge. "I'm DI Yvonne G-"

"Mum! Dad!" the lad shouted over his shoulder. "The police are here."

The DI realised he must be Daniel, Jacky's seventeen-year-old brother. "Thank you," she said, looking at Dewi, who shrugged.

"Let them in." A male voice called from a distant room.

"You better come in then." Daniel took a step back, running one hand through unkempt hair before pushing both into the pockets of his jeans.

Yvonne mused that his trainers had seen better days.

"Mike Bevan." The forty-four-year-old father, with dark hair greying at his temples, held out his hand. Reddened eyes bored into her. "I'm Jacky's Dad."

"I'm sorry to meet you under such sad circumstances." Yvonne accepted the offered hand. "I am so sorry about your daughter."

"Yes, but will you do something about it?" he asked, switching his gaze between her and Dewi.

Yvonne cleared her throat. "Our initial research would suggest Jacky's death was a tragic accident." She pressed her lips together. "The autopsy-"

"The autopsy..." He growled the words. "I really don't care what the autopsy suggests. There is absolutely no way our daughter would have voluntarily climbed into that bin."

"People sometimes do odd things under the influence of alcohol, Mister Bevan."

"Not my daughter, no way... She has walked home many times, and never once climbed into a bin. For heaven's sake, she had no need to. She was twenty minutes from home, and she wasn't that drunk."

Yvonne nodded. "That's something I wanted to discuss with you and with the friends who accompanied her that night. We do not have CCTV footage of her leaving the Cambrian and walking along New Road."

Bevan frowned. "What do you mean?"

"Is there somewhere we can go? It's cramped here in the hall."

"Oh yes, of course..." He rubbed the back of his neck. "Come into the lounge. My wife, Mandy, is in there. I am sure she would like to hear what you have to say."

"Thank you."

They followed him down the hall and in through a door on the left, where a sandy-haired woman sat on a leather sofa, with her head in her hands.

"Mandy?" Mike Bevan placed a hand on his wife's back. "The police are here to talk to us about Jacky's death."

She lifted her eyes to Yvonne's.

The DI swallowed hard at the pain she witnessed within those sunken sockets. "Yvonne Giles," she said, her voice soft. "And this is Dewi Hughes."

The woman nodded, but stayed silent.

"As I was saying earlier, our preliminary findings suggest there was no foul play involved in your daughter's death. I-"

"Your preliminary findings are wrong." The words from Mandy Bevan were an agonised cry that echoed from some dark chasm inside her. "Something happened to our daughter. Someone put her in that bin. Find out who that was."

"Your daughter... Jacky... She wasn't injured. She was fully clothed and there was no evidence of assault at autopsy. Her toxicology results yielded nothing aside from the alcohol she consumed." The DI pressed her lips together. "We have nothing, as yet, to justify a full investigation."

Mike put his arms around his wife. "Well, we know our daughter, and we know she wouldn't have climbed into a bin of her own accord. We know she was murdered. You must keep digging."

"Have family liaison officers been round?" She tilted her head. "They can support you through this."

"We sent them away." Mike scowled. "If the police don't want to investigate, we don't want their sympathy."

"There will be an inquest-"

"We want a murder enquiry set up." Mike stood upright, turning back towards the detectives. "I'll be writing to the crime commissioner."

She nodded. "It is your right to do that."

"And, our MP."

"Of course..." Yvonne eyed photographs of the children on the mantlepiece. "How was Jacky in the weeks leading up to her death? I understand she was home from Manchester University?"

"Yes..." Mike sighed. "It was the start of a four-week holiday covering the Christmas and New Year period. She had been looking forward to it."

"Did she have a boyfriend?"

He shook his head. "Not that we know of, and certainly not locally, if she did."

"What about her friends and social life? Was she happy?"

"Are you suggesting this was suicide?" Mike scowled.

She held up a hand. "No, that is not what I am getting at here. I am simply trying to understand her state of mind, and whether she had concerns about anything or anyone in her life."

"She was happy in herself and didn't seem worried about anything. Jacky was half-way through wrapping gifts for friends and family. The presents are in her room. If she intended harming herself, surely she would have completed the wrapping, and not left it unfinished?"

"May we see?" Yvonne asked, her voice soft.

"If you like..." He pointed to the door. "Jacky's room is the first one you come to, at the top of the stairs, on your right."

"Thank you." Yvonne gestured for Dewi to accompany her.

The bare wooden stair treads creaked as they climbed. The bedroom door groaned open.

"That could do with a bit of oil," Dewi observed.

The DI paused in the doorway, surveilling the former domain of the dead girl.

Although the bed had been made, several items of discarded clothing lay on top of the rose-patterned cream duvet, likely tried and rejected by Jacky on the night she died. The search for the perfect outfit would have been the same for countless young women up and down the country, but not with the same tragic outcome to their evening out.

On the three-drawer dresser, a brush and perfume bottle lay amid an eclectic array of makeup. On the walls, posters of horses sat alongside those of boy bands.

A tiny desk in the corner held note pads, an iPad, and several dogeared textbooks.

A lump formed in the DI's throat as her eyes caught the gifts in the corner. Some wrapped, others not. A roll of Christmas tape lay with a pair of scissors next to the boxes.

"That's a sad sight." The DS pursed his lips.

"It makes little sense to me, Dewi. I cannot tell them, but I agree with her parents. The likelihood of her climbing into that bin of her own volition is slim-to-none. I don't know what is going on here, but something is... And I want to carry on digging."

"You know the DCI won't be happy about us spending time on this... Not without serious questions being raised at autopsy, of which there were none."

She nodded. "I know, but Llewelyn wouldn't need to know right away. I think we should continue to delve into her social media. Let's find out what was going on in her life leading up to this. It doesn't look like suicide, and she had no history of staying out. I want to pursue the case under the radar if necessary."

"Very well." Dewi inclined his head. "I'll support you. Your intuition is usually spot on."

"Thanks, Dewi."

"I take it we won't tell the parents?"

"Not unless we find something. If we do, I will speak to the DCI first, then the Bevans. I don't want to give them false hope."

"Righty-oh."

THE OLD VICTORIAN terraced homes on Kerry Road in Newtown had no front gardens, instead opening directly onto the bend in the main road that led from the railway station.

Yvonne and Dewi parked their vehicle in the overflow carpark near the station, and walked two hundred yards to the home of Peter Turner, the man whose transit van had been parked in front of the bins the night Jacky Bevan died.

Dewi rang the doorbell as they stood tight against the railings to avoid the traffic.

The stocky twenty-six-year-old opened the door.

The DI's gaze was drawn to his belly, where the front of his t-shirt had ridden up, exposing a prematurely developing middle-aged spread. "Peter Turner?" Her gaze was now firmly on his face.

"Yes, that's me... Who wants to know?" he asked in a

gravelly voice, his broad frame blocking the doorway. He made no move to let them in.

"I'm DI Yvonne Giles, and this is DS Dewi Hughes, from Dyfed-Powys police. We're here to ask you a few questions about the parking of your transit van last weekend."

"Why? I didn't park illegally, did I?" He frowned. "There isn't a problem with me parking there, is there?"

"May we come in?"

"I guess so." He ran a hand through short brown hair before turning to lead them down a narrow hallway to his tiny kitchen. He pulled out two chairs from under a small pine table just inside the door. "Did someone complain?" he asked once they were seated.

"No..." The DI eyed him. "Didn't you hear about the young woman who was found dead in the bins behind your van?"

His eyes widened. "My van wasn't there when she was found, was it?"

"No, it wasn't. But it was parked there when she died."

"Oh..." He swallowed.

"We know where it was because we have it on CCTV."

He sighed. "Look, I often park at the back of the fish bar on weekends, unless I am working away. As you can see for yourselves, I have no parking of my own. I tried using the Burger King bays, but they kept moving me on. I am a regular customer of Frances, so she lets me park behind her shop on weekends, when the probation offices are closed and there are more spaces available. During the week, I fight for places along Queens Road."

"So you parked behind the fish bar when? Saturday?"

"Um... Yeah, would have been Saturday evening, when I got back. I think it would have been around nine-ish when I left the van there. But you would know that from CCTV, right?"

"Yes, we have you parking up at seven minutes past nine."

"Right."

"Was anyone else around at the time?"

"Well, the fish bar was still open because it doesn't close until ten. After buying my fish supper, I made my way home. I didn't see anyone behind the shop because, having parked up, I got my food from Frances, who served me herself. I walked across the road to go home, and didn't go back to the van."

"What did you do after getting your food?"

"I took it home. I crossed the road by the traffic lights, walked along the cut-through between St. David's church and the former college, on up through Pryce Jones' carpark, and along the Kerry Road to home. Could you not see me doing that on your CCTV footage?"

Yvonne exchanged glances with Dewi, knowing they did not have footage of him walking home because of the cameras on New Road were out that night. "We will double-check our video," she answered, giving nothing away. "When did you next visit your van?"

"Erm... It would have been Sunday morning. I had to make an overnight trip to Brecon."

"Where is your van now?"

"It is parked outside the Railway Tavern Inn, opposite Queen's Court, literally just a couple of hundred yards down the road from my house."

"Did you witness a girl hanging around the fish bar on Saturday evening?"

"Do you mean the girl who died?"

"Yes, Jacky Bevan... or anyone else who looked out of

place, maybe someone who wasn't buying food at the chip shop?"

He shook his head. "I didn't see anyone."

"Our forensic team may wish to look over your van."

"If you have a warrant, then no problem...And I would want copies of any paperwork." He placed his hands on his hips. "I'm not being awkward, but if you lot go through my van, it won't go unnoticed. People gossip. It could massively affect my courier business. I will need paperwork from you to show that everything was okay, and you found nothing."

"Very well." She nodded, wondering if the DCI or a judge would agree to a warrant to search his van, given there was officially no murder case to investigate.

He checked his watch. "If that will be all?" He asked, eyebrows raised.

Yvonne glanced at Dewi, who nodded. "Yes, we have what we need for now. But if you recall anything else, please call me on that number." She handed him her card. "What is the best number to get you on?"

He grunted before fishing out a dogeared card from his jeans pocket. "That's me: Turner's Courier Service. You have more chance of reaching me on my mobile except for when I am driving."

"Very well." She placed the card in her bag. "Don't disappear."

His smile did not reach his eyes. "I'll try not to."

4

BARRIERS

ifty-year-old Frances Howells tossed a trowel's
worth of chips into the polystyrene tray of a waiting
customer while making polite conversation, her
greying strawberry-blonde hair tied back in a bun.

She shot a glance at Yvonne and Dewi as they entered
her fish bar.

The DI nodded an unspoken message for the shop
owner to continue what she was doing until the queue had
gone. They would wait.

"Salt and vinegar?" Frances upended the salt pot,
pouring liberally over the customer's food.

Yvonne hoped the gentleman didn't suffer from high
blood pressure.

∾

"WHAT CAN I DO FOR YOU?" Frances took off her apron as
she came from behind the counter, leaving her junior
assistant to serve whoever was next.

"We wanted to speak with you about the dead girl you found in your bin."

"I thought so." Frances frowned. "That was a terrible business. I had the shock of my life. You'd better come round the back."

She opened a panel on the counter, allowing them to follow her through the back of the serving area and kitchen, to the door leading out into the car park.

"If you don't mind, I'll have a smoke on the doorstep."

"No, we don't mind." The DI took a step back. "Feel free."

"So, what do you want to know?" The woman asked between puffs. "It was awful... And happening right outside our backdoor too. I mean, why choose our bin to end your life? It's bad for business."

"What makes you think she deliberately ended her life?" The DI inclined her head.

"Well, young women don't sleep in bins even when they've been drinking, do they? And in freezing temperatures like the one that night."

"Did you know Jacky before she died?"

Frances shook her head. "No, I didn't."

"She had never visited your fish bar?"

"Never."

"You seem very certain of that?"

"As sure as I can be." Frances flicked cigarette ash onto the step. "I saw her picture in the newspaper this morning, and didn't recognise her. I usually remember my customers' faces, particularly if they have been here more than once."

"We wanted to ask you about Peter Turner."

"Peter? What about him?"

"We understand he bought fish and chips here on Saturday night?"

"Yes, that's right..." Frances doubled over, coughing. She held up a hand to signal she was all right, before the spasms stopped and she straightened up, wheezing. "I should give these up, I know," she said, holding up the stub of the cigarette. "Type two diabetes, and I enjoy all the things which are bad for me. I never learn my lesson."

"We can all be a bit like that," Yvonne continued to press. "He parked his vehicle here... in front of the bins?"

"Yes, I let him park there. He is a regular customer, and he hasn't got space where he lives. His van is his livelihood. I let him put it here on a weekend when he is in town. He isn't any trouble, and I have known him and his family for a long time."

"Oh?"

"I dated his dad, Phillip, when Peter was still very young... After Peter's mum passed away."

"I see."

"We were only seeing each other for a year, but I felt for the little lad. I have known Peter all his life. He's a hard worker, and a good customer, and he hasn't had it easy."

"How did he seem when he came into your shop that night?"

Frances narrowed her eyes. "Are you asking whether he looked guilty about something?"

"Was he relaxed? Tense? Distracted?"

"He seemed his usual self. There was nothing different about him. He chatted while I prepared his food, then he wished us all goodnight before setting off home with it. I watched him head across the road."

"I see." Yvonne nodded. "Thank you, Frances. I have taken up enough of your time. We should let you get back to your customers. Thank you for talking to us."

"No problem, I'll keep my ear to the ground, and let you know if I hear anything I think you should know."

"Thank you. We appreciate that."

"JUST OUR LUCK for a bloody van to block the only CCTV that would have told us everything." Dewi sighed. "But it's not a crime to park there, and it sounds like he is off the hook."

The DI pursed her lips. "For now..."

THAT EVENING, Yvonne kicked off her shoes as she entered the front door, glad to be home.

"Is that you?" Tasha called from the lounge.

"No," the DI replied.

"Oh, you're hilarious..." Tasha pulled a face as she helped her partner take off her coat. The psychologist was already in blue cotton pyjamas.

"Well, who else would it have been? A burglar letting themselves in with a key, perhaps?"

"It could happen."

Yvonne laughed. "Yes, sure. What's for dinner? I can smell something good coming from the kitchen."

"Thai curry. Are you hungry?"

"I could eat a horse... It's been a long day, Tasha."

"It's got about another twenty minutes to cook. You could grab a quick shower while I finish and dish up?"

"Sounds amazing." Yvonne squeezed her partner's shoulder in appreciation. "Thank you. You know you are too good to be true, right?"

"I know you are one very lucky woman." The psychologist smiled. "Will you have time to meet up for lunch tomorrow?"

The DI grimaced. "Ah, I'm afraid not, Tasha. We're looking into an unexpected death of a young female. And tomorrow might be the last full day I get to spend on it."

"Not a murder, then?"

"I don't know."

"What do you mean, you don't know?"

"We have no evidence that a murder was committed, but a nineteen-year-old female climbed into a rubbish dumpster down a back alley after drinking and passed away. On its face, it's a tragic accident. But something doesn't sit right with me."

"You think someone forced her in there?"

"Something is wrong about this death. I feel it in my bones, but we have nothing to confirm any wrongdoing."

"She had no injuries?"

"Nothing aside from mild bruising and redness, which the pathologist said could have resulted from clambering up and falling in. The bin was around one-third full of rubbish, so she would have fallen about three feet."

"So what gives you the feeling this was no accident?" Tasha tilted her head to study Yvonne's face.

"It's the whole thing. The unlikeliness of it... The place it happened. It was a young woman with no history of ever getting into bins or staying out all night after drinking. All of it feels off. I'd have to take you to the place she was found after dark. See what you think. See if you agree with me."

"We could do that." Tasha nodded. "You say when, and I will go with you."

"Thank you." Yvonne gave a tired smile. "But, not tonight... Right now, I need that shower."

5

NO SUCH THING AS COINCIDENCE

"You'd better grab your coat." Dai ran both hands through his hair. "You were right. Something is going on."

"What do you mean?" Yvonne stepped away from her desk. "Dai?"

"Another body has been discovered in a dumpster... A young male. We ought to get down there."

She pulled her jacket and bag from the back of her chair. "Where? Where was he found?"

"The body was discovered about an hour ago by the caretaker at Newtown cemetery. It is in the bin just inside the gates, next to the stone wall adjoining the cricket ground."

"Oh, God... Does Dewi know?"

"I've just told him. He's going to meet us at the car."

THE SUN, though shining from a naked sky, made barely a dent in the thick blanket of frost covering the ground. It was almost half-past nine.

They parked their vehicle in a supermarket car park, on the opposite side of the road from the entrance to the cricket field and adjoining graveyard.

They held their badges aloft to get through the traffic, which was still a constant on the major route through town, even though a bypass did most of the heavy lifting these days.

The cricket pitch was surrounded by a cordon which extended to the tennis courts and rugby club at the back.

The bin stood to their left as they entered the gates to the cemetery, and was surrounded by SOCO personnel and paramedics. The services of the latter were no longer required, and they passed the DI and her team, shaking their heads in sorrow and disbelief.

"Do we know who the victim is?" the DI asked the uniformed officer stationed next to the tall iron gates.

He nodded. "We think it is twenty-one-year-old Bryn Evans. His parents reported him missing this morning when he didn't return home after a night out with his friends."

"Where is the caretaker?"

He pointed to a man in his sixties who was giving his statement to another constable further along the cemetery path.

Yvonne headed over to them. "DI Giles..." She held up her badge. "Can I speak to the witness when you've finished?"

The WPC nodded, putting away her notebook. "You can speak to him now, ma'am. We're just about done here."

"Thank you." The DI approached the caretaker, who was a good six inches shorter than her at around five-foot-two. "Yvonne Giles," she introduced herself. "I understand you found the deceased?"

The older man's hand shook as he pushed the glasses up his nose and smoothed his white comb-over. "I can't believe it. I had the shock of my life," he answered in a thick Welsh accent. "There I was, tossing some dead flowers and weeds into the bin, and I just happened to look inside it. I don't know why, but I think it was because I had been reading about the young woman found in the bin at the back of the fish bar. I... Well, something made me look. And there he was..."

"I'm sorry," she inclined her head. "It must have given you a shock, Mister?"

"Hugh," he answered. "Hugh Davies... I look after the cemetery grounds. I've been doing it for forty years, man and boy. I'm sixty-three now, and feeling it on mornings like this. It is too cold to be standing out here. I think the lad must have climbed in there to keep warm, like the girl did. It must be some sort of craze that is going on, like with TicTac or something."

"TikTok," she corrected.

"Aye, that's it... I don't know what possesses kids these days, sleeping in bins, you know? It never ends well, does it?"

"What exactly did you see?"

"I saw a brown leather jacket. That's what caught my eye first. I thought it was too good to throw away. I went to grab it, and that's when I realised the young man was under-neath... curled up, like. He looked as though he was sleep-ing, but when I tried to rouse him, he didn't respond. And then I saw his face, and it was all blue, like. It was then I realised he was a goner. That's when I telephoned the police."

She cast her gaze around the field. "What time was that?"

"It was just after eight o'clock this morning."

"Did you see anyone else hanging around here? Or a vehicle, perhaps?"

He shook his head. "Not here... I could see people at the petrol station across the road at Morrisons, but there was no-one around here at the cemetery. And no vehicles or people on the field."

"And you have given a full statement to the officers?"

"I told them everything I did and saw this morning."

"Very well, then. I think you should go get yourself a hot drink." She was about to walk on, but swung around. "If you haven't done so already, I would ask you to offer a DNA swab to the forensic officers over there... In case you left trace evidence in the bin. They can use it to separate your profile from that of any persons of interest."

"Yes, all right." He stared at her for a moment before turning on his heel.

"Yvonne?" Dewi approached her from the direction of the bin, where he and Dai had been conversing with forensic officers.

"Yes?"

"This one is like the last... No obvious signs of foul play but, if you put on some gloves and come with me, I'll show you something I think'll you'll want to see for yourself."

She followed her DS to the bin, where the dead man was still being photographed in situ.

Once this process had finished, Dewi reached for a glass jar which lay between the feet of the deceased.

He held it up. It was lidded, and without a label. Inside was a layer of onion, and a used match.

Yvonne, having donned latex gloves, reached for the

item to inspect it. "It's a mason jar, the kind used for home-made preserves."

"Exactly." Dewi nodded. "And I don't think it can be a coincidence that we have found a jar like this with each body."

"I agree." She gave it back to him and stared at the young man in the bin, lying in the foetal position. "He looks peaceful, like he climbed in to sleep." She shook her head. "What the hell is going on? Is Hanson here, yet?"

"Not yet..." Dewi handed the mason jar to a SOCO officer. "He's on his way, though. They won't move the body until he has seen it in place."

Yvonne frowned. "Two deaths and two jars. One with onion skin, and one with the next layer of the onion..."

"Someone is peeling back the layers of an onion." Dewi rubbed his chin.

"And leaving them for us to find. These jars could be a killer's signature. Perhaps he is telling us that the deaths are connected? Each one representing a layer of a story he is trying to tell? Oh, God... How many layers does he plan on leaving?"

"If you are right, we have to figure out his motive before he reaches the middle of the onion." Dewi frowned.

"We have to work it out before more youngsters die," she agreed.

"What about the match?" Dewi asked.

"I don't know... Perhaps the used matches represent the lives extinguished?"

"Well, if this is the work of a killer, he is one sick son of a bitch," the DS said, swearing uncharacteristically.

"We should get the team together, and look for any connections between these youngsters, and fast. We'll quiz their family and friends. If we can find out what links them, perhaps we can uncover the story behind the killer's onion."

Dewi nodded. "I'll organise a briefing as soon as we get back."

She cast her eyes once more over the body in the bin. The young man's brown curls appeared damp where frost had melted. Had he put the leather jacket over himself? Or had a killer placed it there? She pursed her lips, convinced in her own mind they were looking for a murderer.

THE DI WAITED for the chatter to die down. "Come on, you lot, we have work to do," she reminded them. "Bryn Evans was twenty-one, and had just begun four weeks of a Christmas holiday from Birmingham University, where he was in his final year studying geology. As you know, he is the second person in a week to die from hypothermia, and be found in a large rubbish bin. I want to know why? Why have we found two students who were home on leave in rubbish bins in Newtown? I believe we have a killer in the town who is preying on youngsters who are out for the night with friends. We were already thinking that the circumstances were suspicious, but then we found these..."

She flicked a button on her remote, and a slide appeared on the screen showing the two mason jars containing onion bits and used matches. "Forensic officers are combing through the rubbish and examining these jars and their contents. They have also swabbed and tested the victims' bodies and clothing. There is no sign of sexual assault, and little if any evidence of physical assault. These victims were not strangled, and they had no blunt force trauma. All the evidence is pointing towards death by hypothermia. So why have we found a jar with each victim containing layers of an onion? Skin with the first victim, and possibly the next layer of the onion with the second? Who put those jars there, and what are they trying to tell us? As you can see, a match is also in each jar. Each match was lit and extinguished before it had burned down. A metaphor, perhaps, for the brief lives of our victims?"

She rolled up the sleeves on her white cotton blouse, putting both hands on her hips. "I have to tell you, I don't like this... Not one one bit. I believe these youngsters were murdered, or somehow led to their deaths. The question is how, and by whom?"

Callum cleared his throat. "What if this is some sort of social media craze? Like planking, and the many other mad and dangerous ideas over the last couple of decades."

The DI nodded. "That was a suggestion put forward by the caretaker, Hugh Davies, at the cemetery. And maybe these kids were doing something they had seen others do on social media. That is something I want you guys to look into. Delve into these kids' accounts. Whatever they were on or into, I want it examined. Perhaps they had the jars with them when they climbed into the bins. But forensics found no prints, either on the jars or on their contents. I don't know why these youngsters would have wiped away their own fingerprints, and neither victim was wearing gloves when they were found. So how did they put the jars by their feet while leaving no prints? If this is a craze, then is it one in which we are supposed to be confused by the evidence? I'm keeping an open mind, but I am concerned that we have a killer in our midst, and the perpetrator is toying with us."

"And he is leaving us the layers of the onion because it has significance for him... Like his signature?" Dai leaned back in his chair, hands in his trouser pockets.

"Yes, I think each victim could represent a layer of his story. We solve the deaths, we discover his narrative. So he will continue until he reaches the onion core, or until we figure out what the onion represents, and stop him. So we talk to family, friends, and look through social media profiles to find the link between these victims. If Jacky and Bryn are each a layer of the onion, they have to be connected. If we can find that link, we have a chance of finding the killer before more youngsters die."

She turned her attention to Dewi. "Do we have CCTV for the second victim yet? We need to analyse his movements, and find out if he was followed when he left his friends. We need a timeline as soon as possible. Now, I know the road of interest is once again the main road through town, but I hope the Pool Road cameras had full coverage. What is happening with CCTV footage? Has it been requested? Or were those cameras out as well? We have a lot of information to gather, and we need it fast. There have been only a few days between victims, so we must hurry if we are to avoid another tragic case. In the meantime, I would like uniformed officers to disseminate warnings to pubs, restaurants, and other public places regarding safety at night, and not walking home alone... Especially after drinking. All food vendors, and other places with large bins, should think about locking or otherwise monitoring them until further notice. And... I want everyone to keep silent about the jars and their contents. If we are right about these deaths being murders, only the killer will know about the jars. That is how we will confirm we have the right person when we catch them. So... no talking about those jars to anyone. Am I making myself clear?"

Murmurs of 'yes, ma'am' accompanied the scraping of chairs that marked the end of the briefing.

Yvonne ran a hand through mussed hair. "I have time for a cuppa before my meeting with Hanson," she said, referring to the pathologist.

"Ah," Dewi strode over to her. "He's had to cancel. Something came up."

"Oh no, I-"

Dewi held up a hand. "It's okay, he emailed Bryn Evans' postmortem report through as soon as it was completed. It's in the office, and must have come through during the briefing. I haven't read it yet."

She sighed with relief. "Okay, let's look at it now."

6

PRIVATE INVESTIGATION

Yvonne and Dewi read the postmortem report together. Its findings were like those in the Jacky Bevan case. Though this time, there was blood in the synovial fluid extracted from Bryn Evans' knees, a clear sign that his death involved hypothermia.

Bryn's alcohol level was lower than Jacky's had been. Again, there was no damage to the body, and no finger or palm prints were found on the young man.

Aside from the strangeness of the jar accompanying the body, and the unusualness of two such deaths three days apart, there was nothing to show foul play.

Yvonne sighed, putting the paperwork down on the desk. "Exactly what do we have here, Dewi? Am I looking at this wrong?"

He shook his head. "No, I agree that something about this is off, but I think a social media craze is a strong possibility. Maybe youngsters are daring each other to climb into these things."

"I don't see that happening, Dewi. Why dare someone to do something if there will be no-one there to watch, and it wasn't filmed? Jacky's phone has not been found yet, but absolutely nothing unusual was found on Bryn's. And wouldn't the kids have stopped daring each other after Jacky Bevan's death? If it was just friends having a laugh, they would have stopped messing about after her demise, surely?"

"You have a point." Dewi put his suit jacket on the back of his chair. "But you know what the DCI is going to say, don't you? We have to find something more concrete for him to agree to pouring time and resources into this investigation. If we don't have an obvious case for murder, he may stop us in our tracks."

"I hear you." The DI rubbed the back of her neck. "And we can't mention the jars to anyone in the community. No-one is going to offer information if they don't believe these deaths were murders. We are stuck between a rock and a hard place."

"Our best bet is for you to work on the DCI." Dewi winked at her. "If anyone can talk him round, you can."

"Oh, Lord..." She grimaced. "We've got no chance."

FOLLOWING A SLEEPLESS NIGHT, Yvonne visited the cemetery before going to work. She had risen from her bed at five-thirty to avoid being late into the office.

Her breath froze in the December air as she left her car on the dirt track running alongside the cemetery wall, near the wrought-iron gated entrance.

Remnants of police tape fluttered around her as the icy wind cramped the muscles in her back.

Wearing brown leather gloves, she clicked the latch

open on the gates which towered over her and entered the graveyard.

Immediately to her left lay the large black dumpster. Constructed of galvanised steel, its black paint was peeling off in multiple places and it was still covered in rounds of police tape. The plastic lid was firmly closed.

If the DI had her way, it would have been impounded and scoured for every bit of forensic evidence. As it was, aside from the removal of the various items and bags within, the bin had been left where it was.

She cast her gaze around the tarmac pathways, wending their way amongst the graves and ball-shaped yew trees. Grave stones and monuments appeared to sigh, drooping at various angles because the ground supporting them had subsided. Some had evidently become so dangerous they had been laid down on the earth to stop them from falling and crushing an unsuspecting mourner.

There were other trees besides the yews. Bare cherries, which would blossom like flowery umbrellas in the spring, and behind her, a leafless weeping willow stood alone atop the hill which overlooked the dearly departed.

There were more hills, distant ones, all around her. Beautiful, she mused. A fitting resting place for those beneath the turf. But not the bin. That had no business being a residence of the dead, not even a temporary one. No, that had been all wrong.

She strolled along the path, away from the gates, wondering whether a killer had trodden the same route. Was this the direction from which he had come? There was no CCTV present. It would have been an obvious approach path. Beyond the graveyard, she could see the side of a large Poundstretcher store, its bright red signs and painted fascias stood out against the greenery behind. Off to her left, graves covered the sloping land down towards the traffic on New Road, the other side of which were supermarkets and the businesses on the Lion Works Industrial Estate.

She turned her attention back to the paths in front of her, wondering which route the killer took. Was the young Bryn Evans walking with him of his own free will? Or was he already dead, and being wheeled or carried to the dumpster?

"It's a lovely spot, isn't it?"

She jumped out of her skin. Placing a hand on her racing heart, she swung round to see a grinning man in his late thirties, only three feet away from her.

She took in the greasy brown hair tucked behind his ears, his boney strong features, and crooked teeth. It did nothing to calm her heart. "You scared the life out of me," she accused, her voice stern.

"Sorry," he laughed. "I didn't mean to. It's six-thirty in the morning. I didn't expect to find anyone else here." He inclined his head, his hands in the pockets of a long, creased overcoat. "What are you doing here, anyway?"

She frowned. "I was about to ask you the same thing." She hoped he didn't notice the nervous wobble in her voice.

"I'm following up on a case... I'm checking out a few things."

She raised an eyebrow. "What do you mean, following up on a case?" Her voice cracked, forcing her to clear her throat.

"That student kid found in the dumpster over there. I'm investigating the possibility of foul play." He narrowed his eyes knowingly.

"Really?"

"Yeah." He puffed his chest out.

"And what makes you think it could be foul play?" She asked innocently.

"Well, it looks like the police are treating this like a tragic accident. But..." He cast his eyes about, as though a killer might lurk around any tree. "I think it could be murder." He emphasised the last for effect.

"Really?" She cocked her head. "Why so?"

He shrugged. "Actually, the parents of the dead girl wanted someone to look into her case. They are unhappy about this being signed off as an accident. They want a full investigation. And me? I'm a private investigator with years of experience. So, they felt I might be the best person for the job."

"I see..." She chewed the inside of her cheek. "What was your name, sorry?"

"Tim's the name." He announced, pulling his hands out of his pockets and placing them on his hips. "Tim Owen."

"Well, Tim, you gave me a fright. You should be careful how you approach lone females when you are lurking around graveyards in the early morning."

"Erm, sorry about that." He grinned again, not looking the least bit remorseful. He stepped closer to her.

She took a step back.

"I don't know your name," he said, placing his hands back in his coat pockets.

"Yvonne," she answered, feeling the hairs rising on the back of her neck. She stifled a shiver.

"Are you here visiting someone?" He asked. "Oh, wait... You didn't know the boy, did you?" He grimaced.

"Not personally," she answered.

"Oh, good... I didn't mean to..." His voice faded away.

"I was visiting a friend before work." The DI wasn't sure

of this self-proclaimed sleuth and thought it best to not to give anything away.

"I see. Well, I won't keep you. I've got clues to find." He tapped the side of his nose, implying he knew things he wasn't prepared to share.

Yvonne resisted the urge to tell him she likely wouldn't be interested in anything he had to tell her, anyway. He didn't present as someone with his finger on the pulse. Tim Owen had the aura of a wannabe, she mused, hoping she wasn't being churlish because he was treading on her toes, almost literally. "Well, I cannot hold back a keen and experienced investigator," she answered, turning before he could see the smirk she struggled to hide. The DI didn't know whether to laugh or be afraid. Although she found his antics comical, there was something about him that unnerved her.

She checked her watch before heading back to her car.

7

A FRUSTRATING TIME

She arrived at the office fifteen minutes early, to find Dewi already there.

"Kettle is on," he greeted.

She unbuttoned her coat, setting her bag down on the edge of the desk. "Thanks, Dewi."

"The DCI came through a few minutes ago asking for you." He brushed down the front of his blue cotton shirt and straightened his tie. "I said I would let you know."

"Right, thank you." She ran a hand through her hair. "I've just had an interesting encounter at the cemetery."

"Have you?" Dewi raised his brows. "What were you doing down there? Did you find something?"

"No." She shook her head. "There was a private investigator poking about down there. Some guy called Tim Owen."

"Tim Owen?" Dewi frowned. "That name rings a bell. Oh, hang on, isn't he the guy that looks into benefit fraud cases? There was a piece on him in the paper a couple of years back. He was offering his services to people who thought their partners were cheating on them. He came across a little sleazy."

"I'm glad you thought that." She sighed. "I was wondering if I was being too judgemental. The guy gave me the creeps, to be honest. And he is no respecter of personal space. He came up on me out of nowhere."

"So, what was he up to?"

"Looking for clues," she said, doing an impression of him tapping his nose. "I was expecting him to pull out a magnifying glass and pop on a deerstalker. I swear the man is not the full shilling. He said Jacky Bevan's family asked him to investigate her death. And I have a feeling he is going to be all over it, and us, like a rash. He could be an utter pain in the arse."

"Oh, dear." Dewi grimaced.

"Quite... I think he sees himself as a sort of Columbo, but he comes across more like Inspector Clouseau," she laughed, referring to the bumbling detective in the old Pink Panther movies.

Dewi nodded. "I'm not surprised about the Bevan family. I thought they would push this further. They don't believe their daughter went into that bin of her own free will."

"No, and neither do I, Dewi." She crossed over to the kettle, pouring water on their teabags. "The thing is, we have no concrete evidence of wrongdoing. We can't tell them we agree with their suspicions without telling them about the jars we found. I'll speak to the DCI. I'm worried we will have more victims, and I want his approval to put out an official warning to the local population."

"I hope he listens." Dewi accepted his mug of tea. "Thanks... Dai and Callum are looking through the social media of Jacky and Bryn. I have asked them to update us later."

"Good." She sipped the hot tea. "As soon as I've downed this, I'll go see Llewelyn and ask if we can go public."

SHE KNOCKED on the DCI's door. "You wanted to see me, sir?"

"Ah yes, Yvonne, come and take a seat." He motioned to the chair on her side of the desk. He looked unusually dapper and well-coiffed.

She sat in her crumpled skirt and creased blouse, waiting for him to tell her why she was wanted.

"I'm told Dai and Callum are delving into the social media accounts of Jacky Bevan and Bryn Evans. Is that correct?"

"It is." She narrowed her eyes. "Why do you ask?"

"Have they found anything?"

"I don't know, sir. I haven't spoken to them yet this morning, but they hadn't when I asked them before going home yesterday."

"What are they looking for?"

Yvonne cleared her throat. "Anything that might suggest a reason for the students ending up in large wheelie bins in the middle of the night. If there is something behind these deaths, we should find out what, and warn others." She inclined her head. "I thought the reason would be obvious?"

"Sure." He nodded. "But you think these deaths are murders, I can tell, and I want to discuss that with you."

She smoothed down her skirt, drying damp palms. "I suspect the involvement of a third person or persons, yes."

"Explain?"

"I do not believe that a girl would choose to get into a rubbish bin of her own accord. As I discussed in the briefing yesterday, we found an unlabelled jar at the feet of each of the two victims."

"Ah, yes, the jars with the bits of onion and matches." He nodded.

"A single used match, yes."

"And you think they were left by a killer?"

"I do, obviously. I consider it too much of a coincidence that these jars ended up with both victims. Please tell me you agree with that, at least?"

"Oh, I do not disagree." He held up a hand. "I think the deaths could be connected, but I do not agree this proves there is a murderer on the loose. The teens may have taken those jars into the dumpsters themselves."

"But why?" Her eyes sparked. "Why would they do that?"

"For an as yet unknown reason." He shrugged. "Your DCs may uncover what lay behind those decisions as they sort through social media."

"I get that, but I still feel those jars were left there by a killer. I know I cannot evidence that yet, but I have reasons for feeling as I do."

"The crime commissioner is concerned that we could frighten the community unnecessarily." He cleared his throat.

"So, that's it... There may be a killer on the loose, but until we have hard evidence of that, we can't worry people too much."

"Something like that. Christmas is almost upon us. Local hoteliers and businesses have had it hard over the last few years because of the pandemic. They are hoping to make up some of their losses over the next six weeks. The commissioner is up for election next year. He is worried about getting the blame for any panic, and the resultant loss of earnings, and I can see his point."

"And there was I thinking that our primary concern would be the possibility of finding another young student dead in a rubbish bin. What was I thinking?" She threw her hands up.

"No need to be facetious, Yvonne." Llewelyn sighed. "Look, I see your point of view. I do, and I see why you might be concerned about a killer. But without actual evidence of wrongdoing, can we really expect local businesses to take a hit? Because they would, and you know it. Pubs, restaurants, clubs, and even takeaways could suffer if people are worried they might be murdered and stuffed in a bin after a few drinks. And we really have nothing to justify that fear."

"Can we at least warn people not to walk home alone?"

"Of course, we do that anyway."

"You know, Jacky Bevan's parents do not believe their daughter died accidentally."

"Have you spoken to them?"

"Yes."

"Did you inform them of your suspicions?"

She wrinkled up her nose. "No, but they know their daughter, and that is how they feel."

"It's not unusual for relatives to suspect foul play. It is hard for them to accept an accidental death."

"They've hired a private investigator."

"What?"

"Yes, you heard me right." She sighed. "I had the good fortune of meeting him in the cemetery this morning. His name is Tim Owen. Well, I say meet, but what I mean is he crept up on me. Scared the life out of me. I have a horrid feeling he is going to keep turning up in places we would rather he didn't."

"You say the family hired him?" He frowned.

"Yes, they are clearly fed up with what they see as us sweeping their daughter's death under the carpet. And I can see their point." She folded her arms. "We cannot afford to alienate the families. We need them on board if we are to get to the heart of what is going on."

"Do you think you can keep that PI under control?"

She shrugged. "I don't know. I hope so, but he doesn't strike me as someone who would respect boundaries, if there was something he wanted to access."

"I get the impression you don't like him very much?"

She lowered her eyes. "Well, to be fair, I barely know the man. But I found his sudden appearance and his demeanour this morning somewhat galling."

"That's not like you, Yvonne. You usually have abundant patience for people."

"He gave me the creeps."

"Well, monitor him, will you? And let me know what he's getting up to."

She nodded. "I'll do what I can."

"Have you spoken to the family of Bryn Evans?" He inclined his head, studying her face.

"Not yet. As a matter-of-fact, I was planning to go see them this afternoon."

"Do we know if they have spoken with this Tim Owen fellow?"

She shook her head. "No, but I can ask when I see them."

"Good..." He looked at his watch. "Well, if there's nothing else?"

"That is all, Chris."

"Right, I have a meeting with the Mayor in twenty

minutes." He ran a hand through his hair. "I'll catch up with you later."

"No problem." She left him to it, walking the corridor back to the main office and muttering to herself, worried they might be mere days from finding another dead body in one of Newtown's bins.

THE DI and Dewi arrived at the Cambrian Gardens housing estate around two in the afternoon.

They parked their car by the Jehovah's Witnesses' church on the opposite side of the road and walked to the pale-brick, detached three-bedroom house, whose front garden boasted a mature birch tree and tidy lawn.

They accessed the house via a path made of concrete pavers.

Dewi rang the doorbell.

A teenage girl answered, dressed in jeans and a t-shirt, her blonde scrunched in a loose bun. "Yes?" she asked, a sweet clunking against her teeth.

"DS Dewi Hughes, and this is DI Yvonne Giles. Your mum and dad are expecting us."

"Oh, yes..." She removed the sweet from her mouth. "They are in the lounge with my sister Carol. I'm Bonnie," she added.

"Pleased to meet you, Bonnie." Yvonne nodded.

They entered a sizeable double-aspect lounge, filled with light and air.

Bryn's parents sat together on the couch, his dad holding his mum's hand.

He stood as the detectives entered, running a hand through greying brown hair.

Both appeared to have had little sleep, their eyes puffy, and skin lined from dehydration.

"I'm Bob, and this is my wife Diane," he said, extending a hand towards them.

Dewi shook it, followed by Yvonne.

"We are so sorry for your loss," the DI began. "It must have been an awful shock."

"I don't think it has fully sunk in yet." Bob sat on the arm of the sofa, on the other side of his wife, so the officers could have a seat next to her.

"These things take time." Yvonne nodded.

Carol and Bonnie left the room.

"Our daughters..." Bob sighed. "They will be lost without their older brother."

"How old are they?" she asked.

"Bonnie is fourteen, and Carol is eighteen. Bryn had not long turned twenty-one."

Diane let out a sob, burying her head in her hands.

"Such a waste..." Dewi pressed his lips together, turning his pensive gaze to the window overlooking the garden.

Yvonne took out her notebook. "Do you know if Bryn had ever spent the night in a dumpster before?"

"Not as far as we know." Bob rubbed the back of his neck. "I mean, I can't comment on what he got up to at college, but he never mentioned doing anything like that while he was away. And he has done nothing like that when staying at home with us, either on holiday or when he lived with us."

"I see. Is there a reason he might have chosen to that night? I understand you were expecting him home?"

"I don't know why he would want to spend the night in a bin."

"I'm sorry to ask this, but had there been any arguments at home that day?"

Bob shook his head.

"What about his friends? Were you aware of any issues there?"

"None that we knew of. He was really looking forward to seeing his friends. I am sure he would have told us if there was a problem. Unless... Unless something happened during his evening out."

"Was he in contact with you that night? Did you text with him at all?"

"No, we didn't see the need. He had already told us he thought he would be home by one in the morning. Although he had his phone on him, Bryn wasn't one for doing a lot of texting. And we wouldn't normally disturb him on his night out."

"I see." Yvonne scribbled in her pad.

"How well do you know the friends he was out with that night?"

"We know those boys well... He grew up with most of them. We've had them around here for tea many times throughout his childhood and teenage years."

"Had you any concerns regarding any of them before?"

Bob shook his head. "No."

"Have any of them been in touch with you since Bryn was found?"

"We've talked on the phone, and Alex, his best friend, has been here to give us his condolences in person. He was in pieces, poor lad."

She nodded. "I can imagine. Did Alex have any idea why your son ended up in that bin? Or why he was in the cemetery at all?"

"No... He said it was as much of a shock to him as it had

been to us. He does not know what Bryn was doing there. Will you be speaking to Bryn's friends?" He placed his hand on his wife's back.

"We will be, yes. Alex is coming into the station tomorrow."

"Maybe they will remember something important."

"Maybe..." She put her notebook away. "Can I ask, has a gentleman called Tim Owen been in contact with you?"

"Yes." Bob folded his arms. "He's going to help us look into our son's death. He says he is a private investigator with a wealth of experience."

She pursed her lips. "When did he make contact?"

"Yesterday." Bob narrowed his eyes. "Why do you ask?"

"Is he charging you a fee?"

"He is, but we will pay anything to find out what really happened to our boy. Especially if there is no criminal investigation into his death?" His wide eyes begged her to tell him there would be.

She couldn't confirm it even if she wanted to. And she wanted to.

"We have no evidence to support a criminal investigation at this stage." Her gaze was soft with empathy. "But if that changes, I will be the first to let you know."

"Thank you."

"Did Bryn know Jacky Bevan?"

Bob shook his head. "Bryn watched the news about Jacky with us, and I remember him saying what a shame it was, as she seemed an intelligent, pretty girl from what he could see on the telly. He said he would have liked to have met her. I assumed that meant he did not know her."

"I see. Well, I have taken up enough of your time." She rose from her seat. "Are family liaison officers working with you?"

"Yes, they are." Bob ran a hand through his hair as he rose to see them out. "They mean well." He sighed. "But right now, we need time alone to come to terms with what happened. We want to answer your questions to help the investigation, but the rest of the time, we would rather be left alone."

She nodded. "If you let them know how you are feeling, they will work with you at your pace and give you the space you need." The DI handed him her card. "Please contact me if you hear or remember anything you think might help us."

"I will." He placed the card on the mantlepiece. "I'll see you out."

8

VICTIMOLOGY

"Your guy has been a busy bunny." Dai grinned at Yvonne as she joined her team in the main office.

She raised her brows. "What guy?"

"Inspector Clouseau."

"Tim Owen?" She pulled a face. "Do me a favour and don't call him my guy." She shuddered. "Just... No."

He laughed at her reaction.

"What has he done, anyway?" Yvonne placed her hands on her hips.

"He's appeared on two or three true-crime podcasts, spouting his two pennyworth, and implying he knows a lot more than he can say. The problem is, he is giving everyone the impression he *has evidence* the deaths are murders. He is whipping up powerful sentiment in others who then want to do their own sleuthing. Uniform have spotted a few people with phones on gimbals doing so-called reporting from what they think are the crime scenes. Most of these amateur sleuths are from out of area."

"Oh, God..." She palmed her forehead. "The DCI won't

be happy, and there is bound to be a reaction from the local community."

Dai nodded. "There have been several complaints already. Gardens have been trampled and invaded, and outbuildings, gone through... Bins, too."

"Nightmare..."

"And it is rumoured he has started his own podcast, and is calling it Tim Owen Investigates. So we can expect a lot more of this nonsense."

"Does Llewelyn know all this is going on?" she asked, referring to the DCI.

Dai shrugged. "If he does, he hasn't mentioned it to us."

"Okay, we'll need to monitor Owen and his minions. Please keep me updated."

"Will do."

Something had caught the DC's eye from outside of the window. He strode over to investigate. "I don't believe it!"

"What?" She joined him in peering out.

"It's Tim Owen... What the hell is he doing down there?"

It took a moment for her to locate the hunched figure in the car park. Owen was eyeing the front of the station in between ducking behind parked cars.

Yvonne tutted. "I would tell you I didn't believe it either, but unfortunately, regarding Mister Owen, I am no longer shocked by anything. The man is a noodle, and a pain in the behind."

"Should I shoo him from the premises?" Dai moved away from the window.

She shook her head. "No, it's okay, leave him be. He can't do much harm out there, and at least we know where he is. Besides, you cannot blame people for being suspicious about the circumstances of those deaths. The public has a right to question, though not a right to trample other people's gardens. Our car park is probably fair game, however. If we alienate people, they might keep vital information to themselves. We'll leave him to his shenanigans as long as he doesn't invade the station."

Twenty-one-year-old Alex Pryce attended the station at half-past twelve in the afternoon, apologising for being late, and blaming his tardiness on a flat battery in his dad's spare pickup.

He was dressed in jeans, and a white cotton shirt patterned with tiny grey and black circles. His blonde hair was cropped in a gel-cut, giving him a clean, modern look.

"Thank you for coming in to see us, Alex," Yvonne began, setting her papers down on the desk, and leaning back in her seat. "Do you know why we asked you here today?"

He leaned forward, elbows on the desk, fingers interlinked. "I assumed it was to ask me about Bryn, and what we got up to on the night of his death?" He smoothed the hair on the top of his head.

"Yes, that is pretty-much it." She nodded. "We will probably hand his case over to the coroner for the inquest soon, but I still have a few questions and loose ends I would like to tie up before we do that."

"Of course." He had a strong, confident voice which gave him an air of competence, as though few things would phase him.

"Would you go through the evening for me? Especially from the time you met up with Bryn. How did the night unfold?"

He sat back in his chair, rubbing his forehead. "Erm, we

started off at the Railway Tavern near the train station. I got there just after six. Bryn, Rob, and Simon were already there. I was late because I had been working earlier in the day. I work in a music shop selling instruments on the Lion Works Industrial Estate on New Road."

"That's close to the cemetery, isn't it?"

"That's right, it is only a few hundred yards from the front entrance to the cemetery, across the road."

"Had the others been working that day?"

He shook his head. "No, the others had come home from their various colleges for the Christmas break. They met up at the pub around five o'clock and started drinking early. I'm afraid I can't hold my alcohol as well as they can, so it suited me to join them later. We had booked a table for a curry at nine-thirty and planned to continue drinking afterwards at the Castle Vaults. It was going to be a long night."

"I see, and why had you planned this for mid-week?"

"It was Simon's birthday. We thought about having the celebration on the following weekend, but the birthday boy had planned a getaway with his fiancé, so we had our night out on the actual anniversary."

"I see, that makes sense... How were they when you arrived at the Railway Tavern? Presumably, you were sober at that point?"

"I was, yes. They had necked a couple of pints already by the time I arrived. They were happy, and boisterous maybe, but not drunk at that stage."

"How long did you stay at that first pub?"

"I think we left there at quarter to seven and headed to the Queen's Head on New Road, where we stayed for one pint before heading to the Cambrian Vaults on Long Bridge Street."

She pursed her lips, remembering that the Cambrian

had been the last pub Jacky Bevan drank in before she was found in the dumpster behind the fish bar. "Did Bryn know Jacky Bevan?"

He shook his head. "I don't believe he did, no."

"Are you sure about that?"

"We talked about her death briefly while we were out that night, and Bryn thought it a shame that such a good-looking girl had died that way. At no time did he mention knowing her, and I got the distinct impression he had never met her because of the things he said."

"What about yourself?"

"I thought I recognised her, when I saw her photograph on the news. I think I had seen her out in town, previously... Not for a while, though. The news article said she was a student in Manchester, so she wouldn't have been out in Newtown much over the previous year or two. But I may have seen her about at some point. I just don't remember when."

"Okay... What was Bryn's mood like? Was he happy? Sad? Worried?"

"I would say he was thrilled when I arrived at the Railway Tavern. He was in high spirits. The beers were going down well. His mood was good."

"What about your other friends, Simon Hales and-"

"Rob Jenkins." He finished her sentence for her.

"What sort of mood were they in?"

"They were happy, and having a good time. They got fairly drunk, but nothing out of hand."

"What about later on? Did Bryn's demeanour change at all?"

He tilted his head, his eyes wandering off to the left. "I would say he quietened down later on. We had all calmed down a bit, I would say. We had curry at the Gulshan restaurant on Broad Street, and I probably ate more than I should have. It slowed me down a lot. I think the others were probably similar. We were still enjoying our night, but I think we had simmered down a lot by the time we finished the night at the Castle, though we ended the night on shots."

"Did Bryn show any sign of being in a depressed mood after the shots?"

"I wouldn't say depressed, no. Quiet, yes. He looked tired by the end of the night, and he was quite drunk. None of us had pulled." He grimaced. "Sorry, but that sometimes puts a dampener on things. And Bryn said he'd had enough, and was going home. He left the Castle about twenty minutes before we did."

"I see... Do you think Bryn was drunk enough to clamber into a rubbish bin instead of going home?"

He rubbed his nose. "It's possible... He was unsteady on his feet after the shots."

"Had he ever done anything like that before?"

"What, slept in a bin?"

"Yes, had he ever climbed into a bin before to keep warm and sleep off intoxication?"

"I don't know. All I can tell you is he never mentioned sleeping in bins to me. But look, I cannot speak about what he got up to at college. Maybe it's something he started doing in Birmingham. I wouldn't know anything about that. I can only say that he never discussed doing anything like that with me, and we were best friends. We texted each other most days."

"Perhaps I should speak to his college friends." She gathered her papers together.

He frowned. "Wait, haven't you got CCTV footage from town and New Road? Couldn't you check it to see if you have him going into the cemetery? There are cameras everywhere these days. You might find your answers there?"

"Perhaps..." She would not discuss with him what they did and didn't have. "I think that will be all for now, Alex, though I may need to speak with you again at some point."

"Sure..." He shrugged and yawned, stretching his arms skyward. "Any time."

YVONNE CAUGHT up with Dai and Callum as they trawled through Jacky Bevan and Bryn Evans's social media. "Found anything?" She asked, pulling a chair up to their desk.

"Not yet." Callum sighed. "There is nothing here to explain why Jacky would end her life in a rubbish bin."

"Ditto for Bryn." Dai leaned back in his chair. "I am going through the friends list to see if any are known to us. So far, there is no-one with anything other than a minor criminal record."

"Hmm..." The DI rubbed her chin. "There has to be a connection somewhere. Alex Pryce, Bryn's bestie, stated he knew of Jacky. He claims he didn't know her well, and they didn't move in the same circles, but he had heard of her before. There is a two-year age gap between Jacky and Bryn. But, if Alex was aware of her, perhaps one of the other friends was too? Maybe with a closer connection? I think we should speak to them all." She pointed to the DCs' computers. "Is there anything in those profiles to suggest a direct link between Jacky and Bryn? Did they have hobbies in common? Were they members of the same club now or in the past? Did they go to the gym or somewhere else where they could have bumped into one another? Could there be a more private connection?"

Dai frowned. "Well, if they had struck up a friendship in the past, surely Alex would have known that? Especially if he was such a good friend to Bryn?"

"You would have thought so, unless the victims bumped into each other more recently, like during this Christmas break? Keep digging. I will speak to Karen Jones, Jacky's best friend from school. She is coming in to see me this afternoon, but doesn't think she can tell us anything useful. We shall find out, I guess? She may have seen something while they were out that night and not realised the significance. While you are in those profiles..." She tapped her pen against her hand. "Did either of the victims take part in any challenges? Like the ice bucket challenge, for example."

"Jacky did a no-makeup thing last month," Callum answered.

Dai shook his head. "I have found nothing for Bryn. He was active on the big platforms, but it doesn't seem like he was one to post his every move on them. He was more of an occasional poster, mostly about football or sharing funny memes. There are multiple comments on his page that he didn't respond to, not even with a like."

"Jacky posted a lot: pictures of meals; sharing animal videos; pictures with friends and family, and photos from concerts she attended. There is nothing to show affiliation to any clubs in town, and it doesn't look like she was sporty."

"All right." The DI rose from her seat. "Keep digging until you've gone through everything. I'll catch up with you later."

9

FRIENDS OR FRENEMIES

Karen sat in reception biting her fingernails and watching rain batter the windows.

When someone entered the station or moved through the room, she would squirm in her seat, lowering her head and hiding her face in her hands, as if being there made her guilty of something.

"Karen Jones?" Yvonne, realising the girl was uneasy, called her twenty minutes before the interview was due to start.

"Yes, I'm here." She grabbed her berry-red handbag and tucked a yellow raincoat over her arm. Dressed in pale trousers and a pink mohair jumper, she ambled cautiously over to the detective, shoulder-length mousey-blonde hair tucked behind her ears.

After they were seated in interview room two, the DI poured water from a jug on the table into two plastic cups. "Thank you for coming in to talk to me, Karen. I am sorry, it must be strange coming into a police station when you are not used to it. I want to start by saying how very sorry I am about your loss."

Karen sipped from her cup. "Thank you." Her eyes were on the water.

"I understand you were Jacky's best friend since primary school?"

The young woman nodded. "We were inseparable through school."

"I would like to get to know her better, Karen, and I thought you might be one of the best people to help me do that. I am trying to understand why she ended up in a wheelie bin in a dimly lit car park at the back of a chip shop. Especially since that restaurant was closed at the time we think she climbed in there."

The girl shook her head. "That was so strange to me. I couldn't believe it when I heard. I don't know how it happened. My jaw hit the floor when my mum called me with the news. I thought she must be mixed up, and that it was someone else who had been found in the bin in that car park. It took me all day to take it in. How did my best friend end up in somewhere so filthy? It wasn't like her. To my mind, she must have been scared or desperate."

"From what you are saying, I can guess the answer to my next question, but I will ask anyway. Had Jacky ever slept in a bin before?"

"No." Karen grimaced, bringing her eyes back to the detective. "Never."

"What about at college?"

"She would have told me if she had done something as bizarre as that, and she never did. I don't believe she would have climbed into a bin to sleep, even after drinking. She wouldn't."

"What about for a dare? Or a social media challenge?"

She shook her head. "I honestly cannot see her doing it voluntarily."

"I see... Did Jacky know Bryn Evans?"

"Do you mean the lad who died the following week? No, I don't think so."

"Did you know him?"

"No, but that was weird, wasn't it? The two of them dying like that within a week? I mean, come on... Something has to be going on. Everyone thinks there is a killer in the town, preying on young people."

"The problem is, Karen, there were no obvious signs of foul-play. Both victims died from hypothermia."

"I don't understand how any of this happened. I hear you, that Jacky died from exposure, but it doesn't sound right to me."

"Were you aware of people around you while you were out that night?"

"Sometimes, yes."

"Did you notice anyone hanging around or watching members of your group? Were you followed at any point during the night?"

"I wasn't aware of anything like that."

"Take me through your evening from the time you met up with Jacky, through to the last time you saw her."

"We met at Evie's house on Canal Road. Evie Davies is another friend. We had a glass of wine while we touched up our makeup and waited for Alison Dunbar to join us. I had walked with Jacky from Trehafren Estate. We live within a stone's throw of each other, so we usually walk to town together when she is home from college. My house is in the close next to hers. We set off at six o'clock and walked all the way to Evie's, via New Road and the bridge by McDonalds. It took us about twenty-five minutes to get to Canal Road from our houses. We waited at Evie's, and Alison showed up before seven. After another glass of wine, we went into town around seven-thirty. We began our pub crawl at the Elephant-and-Castle."

"And what was Jacky's mood like?"

"She was having a good time. She was excited to be home, seeing all her friends, and looking forward to a good night out. I remember her being surprised at how quiet it was in town. But that didn't stop her singing as we walked down the street."

"So you started at the Elephant-and-Castle... Where did you go next?"

"We went to Wetherspoons and stayed there for a couple of drinks."

"And how did that go? Was Jacky okay there?"

"Yes, as far as I remember, she was fine: drinking, chatting, telling us about college life, and listening to our stories about town and what we had been up to while she was away."

"And you didn't see anyone watching your group at all?"

Karen shook her head. "No, I didn't."

"Okay, what happened after Wetherspoons?"

"We went to the Pheasant Inn and stayed for over an hour. There was a roaring fire going in the grate, and we were sat at a table next to it. It was cosy and comfortable, and we could hear ourselves over the background noise, so we stayed longer than we thought we would."

"I see. Did anything unusual happen in The Pheasant? I know I keep asking this, but if you put yourself back there now, did you notice anyone paying particular attention to your group, or to Jacky?"

"No, but I have to say, by this time, I was quite merry. I don't think I would have noticed anything untoward unless it slapped me in the face. We were pretty animated in that pub. Probably louder by then too, you know, boisterous."

"Was Jacky lively at this point?"

"Yes, she joined in. We were singing towards the end. The bar man was laughing at us, but only in a friendly way. There was no trouble."

"But you didn't finish the night at the Pheasant, did you?"

"No, we went to the Castle Vaults afterwards, and then the Cambrian, which was the last pub we went to before going home."

"Did anything happen in the Cambrian?"

"No, just more of the same... Except we were probably less lively. By that time, we were all getting tired. Jacky was yawning a lot, and she was the first to say she was ready for home."

"I see, and she walked home alone?"

Karen nodded. "She did."

"Why?"

The girl sighed. "I wish we had stopped her. I really wish we had insisted on phoning a taxi to get her home. We were all short on cash by this time, and didn't have enough for taxis. We could have phoned our parents, but nobody wanted to do that. I really didn't fancy walking all the way back to Trehafren, and Evie offered for me to stay at her house for the night. Evie's flat is only a five or ten-minute walk from the Cambrian, whereas walking home would have taken me half-an-hour. I was sleepy, and quite drunk by this time. And it was cold. I just didn't fancy it."

"So, you stayed with Evie?"

"I did."

"And Jacky walked."

"Evie offered her the couch for the night, but Jacky wanted her own bed. She had walked home many times before, sometimes with me; sometimes on her own. She really had no fear of doing it again."

"What time did she leave?"

"It would have been around eleven-thirty. I wish we had stopped her from walking, or that I had braved the elements and walked with her. I miss her so much."

"I imagine you would." The DI pursed her lips. "But you mustn't blame yourself. Jacky was a grown woman, and it was her decision to go home alone that night. You are not responsible for what happened to her."

The girl shrugged. "I guess..."

Yvonne rose from the desk. "Thank you for coming in, Karen. I will see you out. Please contact me if you remember anything else, or if there is anything you think I should know."

The other nodded. "I will."

∼

YVONNE AND DEWI parked their vehicle in the car park beside Newtown Rugby Club.

Behind them were the tennis courts and club buildings, and off to their left, the barriers and steps at the entrance to the rugby field. Off to their right were the cricket pitch and cemetery. They had entered an area known as the Recreation Ground.

They made their way to the main entrance of the dark-brick rugby club and pushed open the door.

Simon Hales stood as soon as he saw them, so they would know who he was.

"No wonder he plays rugby," Dewi flicked her a glance. "Look at the size of him."

Broad and muscular, Hales had to be around six-feet-five. The DI could imagine him in a strong man competition. He looked like he could lift a tree trunk or two. A shock of ginger hair and freckles completed the all-weather look.

He held out a large hand, which they duly shook.

"I'm Simon," he said, with a Newtonian-Welsh accent. "We are having a pint after practice. Would you like one?" He pulled a face. "Of course not. You're on duty. Trust me to put my foot in it."

He looked older than twenty-one. He could easily pass for thirty-one, the DI mused. His ears were already somewhat misshapen from the many scrummages he must surely have been involved in. And his skin was dry and flaky in places. "I wouldn't mind an orange juice." She reached inside her bag.

"I'll get them." Dewi pulled out his wallet before she could object.

Yvonne turned back to Hales. "Is it all right to talk here?"

"Yeah, we can take a seat in the corner over there. No-one will bother us." His voice was firm and confident. He towered over the DI as they moved to a table near the window. "I know you are here about Bryn..." His words tailed away.

"Yes..." She pressed her lips together. "I am sorry for your loss, Simon."

He sighed. "He was a decent bloke, was Bryn. A good lad... I don't think any of us realised how drunk he was. I mean, he was stumbling a bit, sure. But he'd been like that before, and got home in one piece. We had no reason to think this time was going to be any different. Poor sod... He didn't deserve what happened to him, and I think he had just got himself a girlfriend, too.. back at college, like. I wonder if she knows yet? I don't suppose she's been told.

Bryn said he hadn't mentioned her to his parents. It was early days in the relationship."

The DI made a note. "I'll see what we can do to find her and let her know. The college should be informed anyway, though I suspect Bryn's family will have organised that."

"Yes, I expect so."

Dewi arrived back with two orange juices from the bar.

"Thank you." Yvonne accepted hers from him before turning her attention back to Hales. "So, you say Bryn was stumbling a bit?"

"Yeah... I think he drank between eight and ten pints of lager and finished with a couple of vodka shots. So he was a tad unsteady on his feet. I've seen him worse than that, though."

"Can you take me through the events of the night, as you remember them?"

"Sure..." He recounted their fateful night out, his account broadly similar to that of Alex Pryce, with one major exception.

The DI frowned. "So, you are telling me that Alex left the Castle before Bryn?"

"Yes." His nod was emphatic. "Alex definitely went out from Castle beforehand, yes. He said he was tired, there was no talent left amongst the punters, and he was going home. I thought it odd the way he left in such a hurry, but he obviously had his reasons."

"You are absolutely sure he left first?"

"Yes, and you can probably confirm that with CCTV footage from the pub."

She nodded. "My officers are trawling through that as we speak. Who left after Alex? Was it Bryn?"

Hales nodded. "Yes, Bryn followed ten or fifteen minutes

later, leaving Rob and I downing our last shot before having a final pee and going home ourselves."

"Did you go straight home?"

"Of course." He pulled a face. "Where else would I have gone? I live by the church in Llanllwchaiarn, in the oldest part of Newtown. Since most of the pubs up there closed down a while ago, it is deadly quiet at that time of night. To be honest, I prefer walking somewhere where there is plenty going on. It's eerie when it is so late and silent. I walk faster when going past the church up there, I can tell you."

The DI couldn't help but grin. Here was a twenty-one-year-old man, built like someone's outhouse, and he still felt nervous walking alone in the dark. It was oddly reassuring. "And what did you do when you got home?"

"I said goodnight to my mum. She always waits up for me and makes a hot drink when I get in. After talking to her in the kitchen for ten minutes, I went to bed. I don't even remember brushing my teeth. I was dead on my feet by that time."

"When did you hear about Bryn's death?"

"The following day... It was late when I heard, maybe early evening? My dad told me after the announcement on the six o'clock news. Well, I could have passed out. It was a total shock. Unbelievable... I'm still taking in that he has gone. I remember him in here having a few goodbye drinks before he went off to college. You just never know, I guess."

"It would be a shock, of course." She nodded. "Is there anything else you would like to tell me? Anything you think is relevant?"

He shook his head. "I can't think of anything at the moment."

"Very well then. We will leave you to enjoy your afternoon."

He glanced around at his teammates, who were waiting for him at the bar. "Thanks, I can see that it is my round."

YVONNE TOOK A DEEP BREATH, smoothing her skirt and patting her hair straight before knocking on the DCI's door. She felt more tired than normal. A headache had come on during her talk with Simon Hales and wasn't shifting. Llewelyn had summoned her and, knowing she would only become more tired as the day wore on, Yvonne faced him sooner rather than later.

"Come in."

"You wanted to see me, sir?" She closed the door behind her.

"Yvonne, please have a seat." The DCI sounded as tired as she felt and was dark under the eyes. He was in uniform, buttons gleaming, showing he had either attended or was about to attend an official engagement.

She did as she was told, pursing her lips.

"Are you okay?" He asked, scouring her face.

"I'm fine. Bit of a headache... Nothing to worry about." She leaned back in the chair, glad to take the weight off her feet.

"I've just come from a meeting with the superintendent and crime commissioner."

She shifted in her seat.

"They are not exactly happy, Yvonne." He rubbed the back of his neck, grimacing.

"Really? Why?" She kept her gaze steady.

"There have been several official complaints from locals regarding the influx of amateur sleuths from outside of the area, mostly TikTokers and YouTubers, and the disruption they are causing to people's lives."

"I see."

"And that damned private investigator seems to be everywhere at the moment."

She sighed. "I know he's been hanging around here a lot."

"The problem is, Yvonne, they are trespassing on people's property and damaging gardens. Some of them barely stop short of downright accusing locals of being murderers."

"Oh..." She ran a hand through her hair. "I'll have a word with Tim Owen," she offered. "I'm sure uniformed officers can sort out the social media guys."

"You've been talking to friends of the deceased," he accused.

"Yes I have, what has that got to with-"

"That is part of the problem."

She narrowed her eyes. "Why?"

"To the public, it looks like we are investigating foul play."

"We are."

"No, Yvonne, you are pursuing an inquiry, despite the lack of evidence of wrongdoing."

"I'm establishing the facts, Chris." She sighed. "As you know, I suspect a third party's involvement in these deaths. I simply want confidence in our decision not to pursue this. At the moment, I don't feel confident at all. I am uncomfortable with leaving these deaths uninvestigated."

"Well, like I say, the super and the crime commissioner are not happy. Are you able to keep your enquiries low-key until you can satisfy yourself one way or the other?"

"I thought I was?" She sighed. "I've been talking with the

victims' friends, nothing more."

"Word travels fast, Yvonne, especially on TikTok and YouTube, apparently." He pressed his lips into a thin line.

"Understood." She rose from her seat. "Is that everything, sir?"

"For now..." He smiled, but it didn't reach his eyes. "Go careful, Yvonne."

"I will."

As INSTRUCTED, the DI aimed to keep her enquiries as low key as she could. With this in mind, she set up a meeting with Rob Jenkins, another of Bryn Evans' friends, at his parents' home.

He let her into the three-bedroomed detached house in Stepaside, Mochdre - a rural hamlet at the foot of the Cambrian Mountains, three miles to the south-west of Newtown.

She followed him through to the kitchen.

Although a modern home sporting solar panels and a heat-pump, the kitchen was furnished in a country cottage style with an Aga, copper pans hanging on the wall, and handmade oak cupboards.

He pulled chairs from under the table for them to sit. "My mum and dad are at work, so we can talk without interruption," he said, adding, "Sorry, would you like a drink of anything?"

"No, thank you," she answered, taking in his close-cropped dark hair and wiry frame.

Dressed in jeans and a white tee-shirt, he appeared relaxed, walking around in his socks. "Do you mind if I pour myself a juice?"

She shook her head. "Not at all. I don't want to take too much of your time."

"It's fine," he called back, taking a glass down from an overhead cupboard. "I am on holiday from uni. Time is something I have bags of."

She took a notebook from her coat pocket. "Which college do you go to?"

"I'm in my final year at Hull, studying engineering."

"How long have you been home?"

"Only a week." He joined her with his glass, dark eyes serious as they searched her face. "I am glad you are looking into Bryn's death."

"I want to tie up loose ends and give his family some closure. They don't believe his death was an accident."

"I don't blame them." His gaze fell to the table. "I've had a few sleepless nights myself, wondering how we could have ended the evening differently. When we said goodbye to Bryn, I honestly did not know he would have difficulty getting home." He ran a hand over his hair. "The thought never even entered my head. It's not as though we hadn't had plenty of nights like that before... They never ended up with one of us sleeping anywhere outdoors, let alone in the garbage bin. We always made it home, no matter how out of it we were. And, if I had thought for one moment he couldn't get back, I would have put him in a taxi myself."

"So, you believed him perfectly capable of making his way home?"

"Sure... I mean, he was obviously drunk, but he was talking fine, and walking okay. He was only mildly unsteady on his feet."

"You ended the night on shots, as I understand it? Perhaps the extra alcohol hit his system all at once, after he left you?"

He shrugged. "We've ended the night on shots many a time. And, like I say, he has always arrived home in one piece."

"Could he have had more to drink after he left you?"

"I don't see how. It's not as though he had alcohol with him. I mean, he could have popped into the Queen's Head, I guess, if they had a lock in going on, but you would know that by now. Besides, I don't see how he ended up so far down Pool Road when he should have turned left onto the bridge after McDonalds."

"The problem is we don't know how he got onto that road, either. The CCTV cameras were out for the whole of that area. We have nothing to tell us how he came to be at the cemetery, or even if he went there via Pool Road at all."

"What about his phone? Has that given you any clues?"

"There was no activity on his phone after about nine o'clock. It is still being examined, but if he texted after nine, the messages were wiped."

"Oh..." He rubbed his chin.

"Did he text you after he left?"

"No, he didn't. But I wouldn't have expected him to, really. We would usually text each other at some point the day after, to say what a great night it was or whatever, but not usually after getting home. I know I just crawl straight into bed. We didn't have any idea that something was wrong until we heard the news the following day. It was a helluva shock, I can tell you."

"What time did you get home?"

"Simon and I had one more drink after Alex and Bryn left, and I got the barman to call me a cab. Station Cars took me home. It takes too long to walk. I have done it, but not late at night."

"Who went home first?"

"Err... Alex went first, I think. Yes, Alex was the first to leave the Cambrian. He wanted to be up the following day. I didn't have anywhere to be, so I was in no hurry. That's why I stayed for one more with Simon."

"What time did you get home?"

"Just after one in the morning, I think."

"Is there anything else about the night stand out to you? Did you notice anyone watching your group as you drank in the pubs?"

He narrowed his eyes. "Are you thinking someone did this to him?"

"We have no evidence of someone else's involvement in what happened to Bryn," she parried. "I am merely tying up loose ends; making sure we haven't missed anything."

"I didn't see anyone watching us, but I wasn't looking. Though I would have noticed any ladies eyeing us up. I wasn't checking out guys."

"Were you all close friends?"

"Yes, we are still pretty close. We have all moved on since school. Obviously, we have friends at college and all that. But you never forget your schoolmates, and we had been looking forward to this get-together for a while."

"Is there anything else you think I should know?" She retrieved her bag from the back of the chair.

"No, I don't think so."

"Then I'll be in my way. But I will leave you with this." She handed him her card. "Contact me if you remember anything else, or if you hear something, you think I should know."

"He held the card up." I will.

As she left the home in Mochdre, Yvonne wondered why Alex Pryce had told them Bryn left the gathering first on the fateful night. Alex Pryce would be interviewed again.

10

SOMEWHERE AND NOWHERE

He waited in the shadows, listening to the noises carried on the chill night breeze. He could hear music, and smell the alcohol as he cowered, wondering how long it would be until his quarry left the throng to weave his unsteady way home. And the man would be teetering. He had been in that pub for hours, periodically coming outside with his latest pint to vape and chat to anyone else who was smoking in the open air.

The pub was well lit, smothered as it was in multicoloured Christmas lights, and with a large metal tree in the car park, also festooned with bulbs. That would work to his advantage. He was beyond the glare, in shadows rendered deeper by the bright bulbs beyond.

He hoped not to wait much longer. The cold had penetrated the thick padded material of his jacket. His body ached, his face stung, and the arctic air had given him the urge to pee. The Beast From The East, they called it: the forecasters on the BBC. But it made his grim endeavour easier. His quarry would die faster.

Each time someone left, he ducked. It wouldn't do to be seen. This was likely the only chance he would get to carry out his plan *for a victim who might not be out again before Christmas. Also, there was at least one police detective actively investigating the deaths. Even though the deaths were described as accidents, and the public told there was nothing to see, one dogged detective continued to poke her nose in.*

Finally, he saw the lad stumble out of the pub. Wow, this one really was inebriated. He waited for his intended victim to amble his way beyond the lights, out of sight of the pub's CCTV, stopping and starting as he struggled to maintain balance. Perfect.

THE TEMPERATURE WAS WELL below freezing. Her dashboard had showed minus ten on the drive to Bettws.

As Yvonne left the car, the cold air was still and thick. It hurt to fill her lungs. A vaporous mist hung over the village, giving it the distinct look and smell of winter. Frost covered the grass, rooftops, and trees. Its crystals sparkled in the sunlight, creating a scene resonant with snow.

The pavement was slippery underfoot; it having rained before the freeze set in. The DI concentrated on staying on her feet as she made her way towards the line of emergency service vehicles at the outer cordon.

She lifted the collar up on her coat for protection from the wind and cast her eyes about for Dewi.

"Over here," he called.

Yvonne couldn't see where he was until an arm, waving frantically, caught her attention. She made her way over, flashing her badge at the scene watch officer before lifting the cordon over her head. "What have we got?"

Dewi's expression was grave. "A young lad, around twenty, found inside that..." He pointed towards a large green dumpster covered in police tape.

"Dead?"

He pressed his lips together.

"Oh God, no…" She sighed. "Jar?"

He nodded. "Same story… a clean jar with no label, containing one used match and an inner layer of onion."

She moved closer to the bin. "The next layer… The DCI won't explain this one away so easily."

"We have a serial killer," Dewi agreed. "And the victim doesn't appear to have a mark on him."

"Does Llewellyn know?"

"He's on his way."

"We'll see what he says when he views the scene for himself." She cast her eyes over the wheelie bin, and the two SOCO officers examining the contents. "When was it called in? Who found him?"

"The caretaker for Bettws Community Hall, which is there." He pointed to the large red-brick building behind them. "The bin belongs to them." He pointed to the black and white pub two hundred yards over from them, across a small car park. "That is the Bull and Heifer, the local pub. If my information is correct, the victim spent his afternoon and evening in there, drinking with locals to celebrate his Christmas holiday from college."

Her gaze swung back to Dewi. "Another student?"

"Yes, his name was Carl Jarvis. He was studying law at Aberystwyth. Twenty-years-old."

She winced. "So young…"

"That is the barman over there." Dewi pointed to a tall, dark-haired man in his late twenties, wearing jeans and a faded black tee-shirt. "He served Carl his drinks yesterday."

She nodded. "I'll have a chat with him in a minute. What about the caretaker? Where is he?"

Dewi pointed to the community centre. "He's in there, making cups of tea for whoever needs one."

"Don't let him leave. I want to talk to him too, while his memory is fresh."

"Right-oh."

"Find out if SOCO lifted prints from any of those jars. Tell them I want the items treated with kid gloves. They could be absolutely crucial to nailing our killer."

The DS nodded. "Will do."

THE YOUNG BARMAN stared at her wide-eyed. "I can't believe it... I just can't believe it," he repeated, the knuckles of his right hand gleamed white as it gripped his left. "I can still see him downing his last pint. It doesn't seem possible that he's... that he's..." He fell silent, his gaze dropped to the floor.

"It will be a shock, I know." Yvonne put a hand on his arm. "Are you able to give a statement? I am Detective Inspector Yvonne Giles."

He nodded. "Geraint Jones..." He rubbed his arms, a shiver running the length of him. "Can we do it inside?"

"Yes, of course..." She followed him into the pub, where several people were huddled in the open bar area, shock and concern fuelling their muffled chatter. She acknowledged them with a nod.

Jones led her to a table down the far end, away from the bar. "We'll be able to talk here," he said. "This is a close-knit village. People are in shock." He rubbed his forehead. "I can still see him standing at the bar over there while I served his drinks."

"I know it is a difficult time for all of you, Geraint. Can I call you that?"

"Yes, of course you can. He was well-liked, you know. He drank in here regularly when he was home, and he never had a bad word to say about anyone. They say that only the best are taken, don't they? Well, in his case, it is true. I feel terrible." He leaned over the table, head in his hands.

"Why?" Yvonne's voice was gentle.

"I was serving him all night, and I didn't realise how drink he was. I mean, he must have been more drunk than I thought... climbing into the bin like that. Especially after..."

"After what?"

"Well, you know... after what has happened in Newtown with other youngsters climbing in bins when they've been drinking. It's like it has become a trend."

"Do you think it is a trend?"

"I'd never heard of it before."

"Was Carl on his own?"

"He came in on his own, but that wasn't unusual. He would usually get talking to others at the bar or sit at the wooden tables outside. It was bitterly cold last night, so he stayed indoors for most of the time."

"What sort of mood was he in?"

"He was happy and excited to be home for Christmas. He said he'd felt bored that day. His parents run a stationery business from home, and they had been ultra busy in the run-up to Christmas, but he wasn't depressed or anything."

"How much alcohol had he drunk?"

"Well, he started early. I think he came in just after two in the afternoon and left just before midnight. He had drunk a fair few pints, but he drank soft drinks now and then, and he had a meal here. So he did pace himself. But, by the end of the evening, I knew he'd had enough. I wouldn't have served him any more, but I thought he was fine to get home. Carl only had a short distance to go, but he had to climb the hill. He lived with his parents in Ffordd Newydd, the housing estate just up there." He pointed. "I mean, ten minutes and he would have been home. I just don't get it."

She leaned towards the barman. "Who talked to him last night?"

"The usual crowd... All of them were locals."

"I might take their names from you, if I could?"

"Sure, I can give you those."

"Were any strangers here last night? Anyone you wouldn't normally see? Or did you notice anyone watching Carl in particular? Maybe someone who wasn't drinking as much as Carl was?"

He shook his head. "No... Like I said, it was the usual crowd in here, and everyone was having a good time. There was no trouble, and I saw nothing unusual happening. The only people in here last night were villagers."

"Do you have CCTV outside?" He shook his head. "No."

"What about in the car park? Any unusual vehicles?"

"No, but then there are a few different places to park in the village, including at the community centre next door. There is a lay-by opposite the village shop, and other places along the road. So I can't really say there wasn't a strange vehicle around. Do you think he was attacked by somebody?"

"What did Carl say before he left?"

"He wished the few people who were still here a good night and said he would probably be in again before Christmas."

"Was he walking okay?"

"He was a bit wobbly on his feet, but not overly so. I

thought him capable of getting home okay. He didn't have far to go, after all. I feel bad about that now. I wish I had insisted on someone taking him home."

"Don't blame yourself." Yvonne turned her gaze to the window, wondering if someone had lain in wait beyond the pub carpark, perhaps at the community hall, or near the humped bridge over the brook, in the centre of the village. The pub could readily be seen from each of those places.

"I think that's his mum and dad." Geraint stood, staring through the window. "They are trying to get to the bin."

Yvonne got up. "I'd better speak to them. I can only imagine the pain they must be in." She passed him a card from her bag. "That is my number. If you hear anything you think we should know, call me... Any time."

"Right." He placed the card in his jeans pocket.

AS SHE LEFT THE PUB, she could see the couple pleading with officers to let them go to the dumpster. The woman was crying, her pain evidenced in her wide-open mouth and forlorn stare. "Please," she begged. "Just let me see him."

The woman's husband held her back, the muscles in his face tense, his eyes glistening with tears.

Yvonne approached, her heart aching for them both.

"Are you Carl's parents?" She tilted her head, her gaze soft with empathy.

"We are," the man acknowledged. "We just got here. My wife wants to hold our son. We only want to touch him."

"I know, I'm so sorry, but we have to treat this as a crime scene until we know what happened, and that means preserving the evidence. If there has been wrongdoing here, you would want the perpetrator caught, wouldn't you?"

"Yes..." The man held his wife as she broke down on his shoulder.

"I wish it could be different, but we need to protect the integrity of DNA and fibres, amongst other things. I hope you understand."

"We understand." Carl's father nodded. "We'll stay close until he is moved though, if that is okay? We want to be where he is."

"That should be fine, but you will have to wait beyond the inner cordon. I'm so sorry."

The couple slowly moved back, allowing the plastic-suited SOCO officers to get to work.

Yvonne hoped that victim liaison officers would soon be on hand to help Carl's parents as she left them. Her mission now was to speak with the community centre's caretaker.

She found him in the main hall, moving chairs and tables around so emergency service workers could come in for a cup of tea and a biscuit.

He stopped working as she approached, turning to give her his full attention. "Are you here for a hot drink?" He had his glasses on top of his head of white hair, shirt sleeves rolled up, and he smelled faintly of sweat from the graft of moving furniture.

"No thank you," she answered. "Are you the caretaker?"

"I am. Geraint Jones is the name... And you are?"

"DI Yvonne Giles, I'll be investigating Carl Jarvis' death. I understand it was you who found him?"

"It was, yes." He let out a juddering sigh. "It was the shock of my life, I can tell you. I only wanted to empty the kitchen rubbish. I took the bag out to the wheelie bin, and there he was. At first, I thought he was sleeping. His eyes were closed, and he looked peaceful. I assumed he had drunk a little too much last night and slept it off in the warmest shelter he could find. But when I called out to him and prodded him with my broom, there was no response. That was when I noticed his lips were blue and his body felt hard when I poked it. I knew he was dead. I phoned the police right away."

"Was anyone else here when you found him, either walking around or in a parked vehicle? Or was anyone leaving the car park?"

He shook his head. "I saw nothing, aside from the occasional car driving through the village, as they usually do. We are on the principal route between Newtown and Tregynon."

"What time was this?"

"When I found him? It would have been about eight-thirty this morning." He held his hands in front of him. "Look, I'm still shaking."

"I understand. It must have been a terrible shock."

"I don't really know what to do with myself, and I didn't want to go home after I found him. I didn't want to be alone with my thoughts. So, I stayed here, and have been making tea and coffee ever since, and helping where I can."

"That is thoughtful of you." She turned as firm footsteps approached from behind.

DCI Llewelyn strode towards them. "Have you got a minute, Yvonne?"

Geraint took hold of the broom that had been leaning against the table. "Right, I'd better get on."

She joined the DCI. "You heard the news, then?"

"I did," he answered. "I came as fast as I could. This is the third victim in two weeks. What is going on?"

"Have you spoken to Dewi?"

"I have."

"Did he tell you about the jar?"

"He mentioned there was another one. It seems you were right after all. A third person or persons are involved with these deaths."

"I believe someone knows something." She ran a hand through her hair. "But are they trapping the youngsters in bins, or are they persuading these kids to spend the night in them? The answer lies in those jars, I am sure of it. They are the killer's signature. Each of these deaths represents a piece of his sick puzzle, and he is waiting for us to put it all together."

"Are the victims connected?"

"I think they must be but, so far as we can tell, there is no direct link between them. Whatever the connection is, it has to be indirect. They are all students, but that is not it. There is an overarching narrative here. That is the significance if the onion layers. The killer is waiting for us to uncover it."

"Are you talking to the families?" He opened the flaps of his mac, pushing his hands into his trouser pockets.

"We are, and my intuition is telling me the answer lies with them."

"We have a lot of work to do." He sighed. "We can't have any more deaths, Yvonne."

"We should warn the public and get posters up in all the bars. The forensic results will be available soon for Jacky and Bryn. We may get something from those. In the meantime, the team will keep digging for the connection between these victims, and figure out what is going on in this sick bastard's head."

Llewelyn checked his watch. "Right, I've got a meeting with the superintendent in twenty-three minutes. I had better get back. Will you be all right with this?"

"Yes, you go." She nodded. "I want to speak with the victim's parents."

CARL'S PARENTS returned home when their son's body was taken away, reassured they would see him prior to his postmortem.

Yvonne and Dewi joined them in their three-bedroom semi-detached home in Ffordd Newydd.

The detectives removed their shoes before stepping onto the cream carpet in the hall.

Tom Jarvis led them through to a lounge occupied by two sofas and a long oak coffee table. A large window over-looked the garden and a leafless silver birch.

He appeared lost, looking this way and that, as though unsure what to do with himself. "Would you like a cup of tea?" he asked, finally.

The two detectives answered at the same time. Yvonne said no, thank you. Dewi uttered yes, please.

Tom Jarvis paused for a moment, a look of confusion on his face, before turning on his heel and heading for the kitchen.

Mary Jarvis didn't look at them, but continued to cry, lost in her own thoughts, memories, and self-recriminations.

The DI understood only too well the roller coaster of emotions. Her heart went out to the mother.

The couple appeared to be in their mid-forties. Mary looked two or three years younger than her husband. Their home was small, with a minimalist decor which included pieces of tribal art collected, perhaps, on their travels over the years. The wall opposite the detectives held a mural composed of watercolour paintings.

Tom returned with a tray, which he placed on the oak coffee table.

Although Yvonne had declined out of politeness, she was thankful he had brought four mugs with the teapot. She hadn't had a drink since leaving the house that morning. It was now two in the afternoon, and she was parched.

"Thank you for agreeing to see us this afternoon, so soon after such dreadful news." Yvonne cleared her throat. It was never easy finding the right words. All seemed inadequate at such a time. And opening lines were the hardest of all to get right, if there ever was a *right* in these situations. "If we are going to find out what happened to your son, we need to know a little more about him and your family."

"You think this is something to do with us?" Tom asked, eyes wide.

"No, but we believe his death is linked to other similar deaths in recent weeks. We are investigating how they happened, and what connects the victims. This could relate to any aspect of their lives, perhaps social media, friends, family, or college. But we believe these deaths are connected somehow."

"Somebody must have made our boy get in that bin." Tom flicked a glance at his wife, as though looking for her to back him up. "He didn't have far to come home, and he has never climbed in a bin to sleep before. I had thought about going with him to the pub, but we have been so busy with the business, what with the run up to Christmas, that I decided not to. I can't tell you how much I regret that now."

"What is it you do?" Yvonne took out her notepad.

"My wife is a watercolour artist. She paints pictures, letter paper, wrapping paper, cards, and many types of stationery. We run a business selling these items on websites, including our own. We have been through one of our busiest periods ever, and when Carl asked me to go down to the pub with him, I told him I couldn't because of helping Mary package the many Christmas items we had on order. I wish, wish, wish I had gone with him yesterday."

"Were you concerned when he didn't return home last night?"

A tear fell from his nose. "We didn't know until this morning. It wasn't unusual for carl to stay out until the small hours, especially when he got talking to people. We were exhausted after our busy day, and were in bed at ten-thirty. Bettws is a small village, and so we rarely lay awake worrying when Carl popped down to the pub. The next thing we knew, it was eight in the morning, and we got up to make breakfast. Mary called Carl to come down for his, as she would normally do, and there was no reply from his room. That is when I ran up to check on him, and realised his bed hadn't been slept in. I texted his phone and got no answer, so I tried ringing it, but it was dead. I was about to call the police when I received the call from Geraint at the community centre to say that he had just telephoned the police, and that I should go down there. He didn't want to tell me about Carl over the phone, but I knew... I knew it had to be something to do with our boy, and why he was missing. He eventually admitted to having found him in the bins. We got dressed and went straight down there."

"Did Carl contact you yesterday? While he was at the pub?"

Tom shook his head. "He didn't, but that wasn't surprising because he knew we were busy, and he was considerate that way."

Mary let out a sob.

Yvonne paused, her heart going out to them both in their gut-wrenching grief.

"Do you think our boy was murdered?" Tom asked, finally.

The DI weighed her words carefully. "We'll know more once we have the results of the postmortem. We have little to go on at this stage, but we have recovered Carl's mobile phone, and will hang into it for the time being. Forensics will examine it, along with other evidence. I hope to have a better idea of where we are working after that. I can tell you that there were no obvious signs of violence on your son."

Tom ran a hand through his hair. "That is something, at least. I couldn't bear to think he suffered. Maybe he simply fell asleep?" He looked at her, his eyes pleading for confirmation this might be the case.

She swallowed. "Perhaps he did."

He appeared to take some comfort from that, his face relaxing.

"Had you heard about the two students from Newtown?" Yvonne tilted her head.

"The ones who died like Carl? We didn't know about them until today. We were so busy with the business that we had watched little news for a while. That must sound baffling to you, but we have had a lot of late nights and early mornings, and there were only the two of us doing the packing. I wish we had paid for help, but we thought we could do it on our own. One of Mary's designs blew up on the web, and that painting alone sold well over three hundred copies. Its popularity spilled over into the rest of the business, and with Christmas around the corner, we struggled to keep up. Bryn offered to help, but we wanted him to relax and enjoy himself. We insisted on it. Little did we know that he..." His voice trailed away.

"Nobody could know what would happen here in your village." Yvonne felt for him. "Don't blame yourself."

"If I had known earlier about those Newtown students, I think I would have gone with Carl to the pub to make sure he came back safe. Or I would have texted him to make sure he was okay."

"I understand." She nodded. "Officers from Victim Liaison will be with you shortly. I know there is nothing we can say to lessen the pain, but they will support you and help you navigate the tough days ahead." Yvonne rose from the sofa, followed by Dewi. "And if you need us for any reason, this is my number." She handed Tom her card. "I want you to know that we will do everything in our power to find out what happened to Carl. If foul play was involved, we will stop at nothing to catch the perpetrator and bring them to justice."

"Thank you." He accepted her card before blowing his nose into a hanky. "I'll see you out."

As THEY EXITED onto the Jarvis's garden path, the DI caught sight of someone ducking behind the hedge. She signalled silently to Dewi, informing him of the intruder, before running down the path to catch him.

Tim Owen stood up, straightening his coat, adjusting his wide tie, and clearing his throat.

"What on earth are you doing?" Yvonne asked, one eyebrow raised.

"Er... I came to see how the Jarvis family are doing," he muttered, smoothing his wind-blown hair.

"Do you know them?" she asked, moving closer.

"Not exactly. "

"Then why are you here? This is a bad time for them."

"I know. That is why I came. They may need my services."

She narrowed her eyes. "You should be careful. If this becomes a criminal investigation, you don't want to be accused of obstructing justice."

"I'm not trying to interfere with your inquiry. I am conducting one of my own. It's not illegal."

"How did you learn about this so quickly?"

"A villager rang me. They follow my true crime podcast."

The DI resisted the temptation to roll her eyes. "Don't go trampling on potential crime scenes," she said, walking with Dewi to their vehicle.

"I don't trust him, he's shifty." Dewi flicked a glance behind at Owen, who continued up the garden to the Jarvis's front door.

"I still have him as Inspector Clouseau in my head." She grinned. "I think he is probably harmless enough, but we should keep an eye on him. I get the impression he would go to any lengths to make the extra buck, and I admit there is something creepy about him."

"I can't take to him." Dewi pulled a face. "I don't like how he injects himself into the investigation, hanging around the families like that. There is something ghoulish about it."

She nodded. "I don't like it either, but he's right... It's not illegal to offer his services as a private eye. But we will watch him, and if he puts one foot out of line, we'll haul him in for questioning."

11

JACKY BEVAN

Evie Davies attended the station to discuss her last night with Jacky Bevan.

Yvonne took her to the interview room and waited as the ash-blonde removed her coat, placing it over the back of her chair along with her bag.

Casually dressed in jeans and a blue fleece, she shuffled in her seat, chewing her nails as the DI organised her papers.

"Evie, can I call you that?" Yvonne set her pen down.

The girl shrugged. "Sure."

"I'd first like to say that I am very sorry you lost your friend in such tragic circumstances. It must have been quite a shock."

Evie clasped her hands together on the table. "It's been ten days, and I am still trying to take it in," she said, in a deep voice that belied her slight stature.

"I understand you began the night with drinks at your house?"

"That's right, Jacky and Karen arrived a little before Alison, and we all drank wine at mine to kick the night off."

"What time was that?"

"We had our first glass just before seven, and another one after Alison arrived. We went into town about half-seven-ish."

"What happened then?"

"We started off in the Elephant-and-Castle, and moved on to Wetherspoons."

"Did you notice anyone following you? Anyone hanging around, or making you feel uncomfortable? Anyone paying particular attention to Jacky?"

Evie thought about it for a moment. "No, I don't think so." She paused. "It's difficult to say, really. We always had attention from guys when we were out. Four girls together, we were bound to. But I wouldn't say that any of it was out of the ordinary that night, or worrisome. Nothing stuck out to me. Men said hi, and some of them chatted for a while, but no-one made us uncomfortable. There were few people out in town that night. It had been quiet for a while. I think the pandemic knocked Newtown nightlife back, and it hasn't fully recovered."

"Did you know the males who spoke to you?"

"Some of them; I'd seen most of the guys around before."

"What about the ones you hadn't seen before? Would you recognise them if you saw them again?"

"Maybe I would? I don't know. I don't have a memory for faces, I'm afraid."

"How did Jacky appear to you? What was her mood like?"

"She was happy; brimming with joie de vivre and enjoying being home and seeing us. It had been a while since we were all out together. We were having a good laugh."

"Did anything cause you concern that night?"

"Not at all; that is why I was so shocked to hear Jacky ended up in that bin. That wasn't right. Something bad happened to her. You must look into it. There is no way she would have climbed into that thing. I think someone put her in there. Maybe they held the lid closed or something. Maybe they knocked her out before putting her in there. But somebody did something to her. That is the only explanation that works for me."

"I understand you finished up at the Cambrian?"

"Yes, I think we were all really merry by then, so we were louder than we had been all night; singing and mucking about. The barman was staring at us at one point, so we quietened down for a bit, but he was laughing with us later on."

"Did you watch her leave the pub?"

"No, we didn't. We finished our drinks over the next ten or fifteen minutes while Alison waited for her cab. Then Karen and I walked back to my place on Canal Road, as she was staying the night at my house. She didn't fancy the walk home, and we were pretty-much out of money by then."

"Why didn't Jacky share the cab with Alison?"

"Alison lives in Kerry village, which is the opposite direction to Trehafren."

"I see."

"The last time I saw Jacky alive was when she turned to wave at us before walking out of the Cambrian. I keep seeing her leaving in my mind... replaying it over and over; wishing we had done things differently. I should have insisted she come back to my place instead of walking home."

"You mustn't blame yourself, Evie." The DI tilted her head. "Jacky made her own choices that night, as she had done many times before. Neither of you could have known what would happen."

As she rose to leave, Evie turned back to the detective. "You will find out what happened to her, won't you?"

Yvonne nodded. "I promise we won't rest until we know the truth."

ALISON DUNBAR ATTENDED the station in purple Doc Martin boots, a hand-knitted skirt in multi-coloured horizontal stripes, and a navy-wool hoodie. Her dark hair was long and braided, she had several piercings in her ears and a single stud in her nose.

As the girl plopped herself down in the chair opposite, the DI caught a whiff of incense.

"Thank you for coming in, Alison," Yvonne began. "How have you been?"

The young woman shrugged. "Up and down, mostly down." She fiddled with one of the small rings on her right ear.

"I am sorry about the loss of your friend. It must have been a nasty shock."

"I think Christmas is ruined for everyone." Alison stared at the table, her gaze wistful.

The DI ran through the events of the night with her, confirming what the other friends had recounted, with one exception: Alison remembered a stationary van revving its engine on New Road as they approached the Cambrian.

Yvonne leaned forward, her forearms on the table. "What van? Can you remember anything about it?"

"Its headlights dazzled me, like they were on full beam. I think it was pale, maybe white or grey? I didn't notice the make or model, and it wouldn't have meant anything to me if I did. Vehicles are not my forte, I'm afraid. I couldn't see who was revving the engine because the headlights were so bright."

"No-one else mentioned this van to me." The DI rubbed her chin.

"I'm not surprised. The others were busy singing and laughing as we were going into the Cambrian. I had been rooting through my bag, panicking because I thought I had lost my phone, so I was a few paces behind the others. I found the phone, gave the noisy driver a hard stare even though I couldn't see him because of the lights, and followed the others into the pub. After that, I forgot all about it."

"What about when you left the Cambrian? Was the van still there?"

She shook her head. "I don't think so. It wasn't making a noise, if it was. I didn't look for it, to be honest. But if it had been there, revving its engine, I would have noticed it while I was getting into my taxi."

"Did you text Jacky after you left the pub?"

"No, I went home and talked to my mum for a bit because she was still up, and then went to bed. Next thing I knew it was eight o'clock the next morning, and mum was calling me down for breakfast."

"When did you realise Jacky was missing?"

"Not until I checked my text messages later that morning. Jacky's mum and dad had been ringing around trying to find her. It was Karen who texted me to ask if I knew anything. Jacky's parents were at her door to see if she was there. I texted Evie, and Karen had already been in contact with her. None of us knew where Jacky had gone. As far as we were aware, she went straight home. When we realised she hadn't, we knew something serious must have happened. She didn't have a boyfriend in Newtown, and we knew she had been alone that night. We were anxious, and so were Jacky's parents. In fact, they were frantic. We all went to town, and walked the route she would have used to get home, to see if we could find anything. There was no sign of her anywhere. By then, you guys had already been informed. I could tell by the increased police activity."

"Did you see a van hanging around the next day? Like the one you had seen the night before?"

Alison shook her head. "None that I noticed. Though I am fairly sure I wouldn't have recognised the one from the night before, anyway. I had only seen it in the dark."

The DI nodded. "Did you see any vans outside of the fish restaurant, down the road from the Cambrian?"

"No, but I wasn't specifically looking for one. I'm sorry. Besides, tradesmen are always stopping at that chip shop for their lunch and snacks, so it wouldn't have stood out to me, anyway."

The DI slid her card across the table. "Alison, if you remember anything else, or if you hear anything you think is relevant, please call us."

The girl slipped the card into her bag. "I will. I hope you find out why Jacky ended up in that bin. She didn't deserve to die, and definitely not like that. She was one of the best."

"We'll do everything in our power to understand what happened," the DI affirmed, as she rose to show Alison out, adding, "stay safe."

12

KILLING THEM SOFTLY

Yvonne flicked through her slides, as she waited for the room to quiet down as CID and uniformed officers settled into chairs, ready for the briefing.

She had spent the night before going over everything in her mind; so much so, she had barely managed five hours' sleep as her subconscious mulled over the student deaths, wondering what linked them.

Finally, the room fell silent, aside from the occasional cough.

The DI turned her attention to the waiting officers. "Thank you all for coming. I'm sure I don't have to tell you how serious this is. I think everyone is aware of the suspicious circumstances around the deaths of these three young students." She pointed to the projection on the whiteboard, where the names and basic details were displayed. "Each died of hypothermia, with no evidence of assault, but there is an underlying story here. Someone had a hand in these deaths, and I believe the perpetrator wants us to figure out why they had to die."

She continued. "Three deaths. Three bodies in bins.

And these..." The next slide showed the jars found with each of the dead youngsters. "These mean something to the killer, and he has challenged us to discover their significance. Each one contains an onion layer, and a used match. Each victim was found with a progressively inner layer of the onion. I believe the killer is using this onion as a representation of his story; his reason for killing the victims. It suggests he knew or knew of the students before he murdered them. He is connected to them. Or, perhaps, he didn't know them directly, but had his own student hopes dashed, and hates them for being successful. Whatever his reasons, he wants his story known. But he will not make it easy for us. If he isn't stopped, he will continue killing until we figure out what he is trying to tell us. The jars and their contents have been analysed, and no prints, fibres, or other trace evidence has been found. The jars were sterile aside from their contents." She placed the remote on the table next to the projector. "I'm now going to hand over to Dewi, who will take you through the CCTV and forensic data we have so far."

Dewi took off his suit jacket, placing it over the back of his chair before striding to the projector.

He cleared his throat. "Some of this information is hot off the press. Or rather, hot off the email server. Hanson and his team have been hard at work, and discovered that each of the victims had their faces washed before being placed in those bins. The same soap was used in each case. And, when I say the same, that is exactly what I mean. The chemical traces were identical. When the victims' hands were examined, no soap with that chemical signature was found. This strongly suggests someone other than the students washed their faces. The question is, why? Was it to wash away traces of a chemical used to subdue them? Or to wash away traces of himself? Or was the face-washing part of a ritual? Forensics are working to identify the soap brand."

He changed slides. "On two of the three victims, they found fibres which appear to be from a blue carpet. The fibres were identical, and suggest the bodies lay in the same location for a time, prior to being placed in the bins. Keep your eyes open when out and about. Pay attention to blue carpeting at suspect locations."

"Did they find foreign DNA?" Callum asked, leaning back in his chair.

Dewi shook his head. "That's a negative... Whoever handled those students did so with extreme care not to leave any trace of themselves. They likely used gloves, and may have worn some type of overall. If we are right, and this killer is connected to these students, we need to find the link. Talk to as many people as you can. Talk to your contacts; pick their brains while you are out and about. Have they heard anything? What is the gossip around town? What you mustn't do is mention the jars left with the bodies. We are keeping those under wraps for now for obvious reasons. I'll hand you back to Yvonne." Dewi passed the remote back to her.

"Thanks Dewi, that's about it, except we'll be maintaining a large police presence in town, and an increase in patrols through the villages. Increased visibility will help calm public nerves and hopefully deter whoever is behind these deaths from killing again. Remember, something connects these victims. What is it? Interests? An individual? Families? Something in their past? What? I want all of this researched. As much information as you can gather. Let's get to the centre of this onion before the killer does. I want no more victims."

ROGER HANSON PEELED off his latex gloves and face mask, while giving instruction to an assistant as she wheeled away the covered remains following autopsy.

Yvonne placed her bag and coat on a hook near the main entrance and waited for him to see her.

"I'm sorry to keep you." He smiled, the rims of his eyes red from the intense focus with which he had worked on the victim. He took off his white coat and opened the door for her to enter the office ahead of him.

"I'm sorry. I'm a little later than I intended." She sat in the first of two comfortable armchairs next to his wall of books. "We held an in-depth briefing this morning; there was a lot to go through."

"No problem..." He slid a mug under the nozzle of the coffee machine and pressed the button. "Would you like one?" he asked, turning to her.

"I would love one." She nodded. "A latte, if you do that?"

He grinned. "I do, but only a machine version."

"Anything would be welcome at the moment." She accepted the mug from him. "I haven't had five minutes since leaving the house this morning."

"Well, now you can breathe." Hanson grabbed his drink from the machine, and a clipboard from the desk containing handwritten notes made by his assistant during postmortem.

He sat in the chair next to hers. "It is not safe to be a young student out at night in Newtown at the moment, is it?" He pursed his lips.

"No." She shook her head. "Someone has most definitely got it in for them."

Hanson smoothed his beard, perusing the notes. "If

there is a killer, and I think we are now in agreement, there is. He uses their inebriation to his advantage. I know that sounds obvious, but I don't just mean in order to subdue them. It helps him with his method of killing. They are drunk, therefore their blood vessels are dilated, and they lose heat far faster than they would if they hadn't been drinking."

"So, you've confirmed Carl Jarvis died from hypothermia like the others?"

He nodded. "I have. There is no obvious damage to the body. All physical signs point to hypothermic death, and the lack of damage to the hands suggests the victim did not wake up at any point."

"But you confirmed this morning his face had been washed?"

"It had, but I think the victims are being subdued with chloroform. I have found chemical traces in the tissues and bodily fluids."

Yvonne's gaze turned to the window, and the trees moving in the breeze. "Although he's killing them, it feels like it isn't personal." She rubbed her forehead. "What am I trying to say here? He's not using violence, other than the force needed for initial capture, and perhaps the repeated use of chloroform to keep them under until they no longer wake up."

Hanson nodded. "That fits the physical evidence. But he must be keeping them somewhere until they are dead before disposing of them in bins."

"So, what is his point? It's like he wants to murder his victims, without their knowing anything about it. Killing them softly, if you will. It's the opposite of what we would expect from a serial killer." She brought her eyes back to Hanson. "I think he is murdering these youngsters as a way of harming someone else, or maybe the community at large. Those kids are merely a means to an end. He doesn't wish them harm, per se."

"Hence the goodie jars that form part of the narrative. He can't punish anyone if the intended targets don't know the deaths are murders."

"Exactly. His signature is the only way of telegraphing to the world that he is killing, without the need to desecrate the victims. Maybe it pains him to harm the kids? But then, why do it? What is the story behind it? What are we supposed to work out?"

"Whatever the story is, it is of primal importance to him."

"Agreed." She pressed her lips into a thin line. "Maybe he is harming the young to punish the old?"

"I'll have the report typed up before I leave here today, all being well, and certainly by lunchtime tomorrow. I will send it to you as soon as it is done."

"I'd appreciate that, thank you." She finished her coffee. "I'd better get back to it. I think we need a profile of this killer as soon as possible." She rose from her seat. "I'll look forward to your report."

13

PROFILE OF A KILLER

"All right, what are you doing?" Yvonne stood, hands on hips, her frustration evidenced by the stern look and flared nostrils.

Tim Owen straightened up, brushing down his crumpled mac. "I thought I dropped my car keys here. I am looking for them." His face flushed with colour.

Yvonne cast her eyes around the station car park as she locked her car door, checking there was no-one else lurking about with the private eye.

She didn't know whether to laugh or cry. "How are we supposed to concentrate on the job in hand, with you running around like Inspector Clouseau? This isn't a Pink Panther movie, it's a serial murder investigation. What on earth are you up to? And don't repeat that you are looking for your car keys. I don't believe it for one moment. It's bad enough that we have the local press camped on our front steps, without you doing... whatever it is you are up to?"

"I wanted to see what you were up to, actually." He shrugged.

"Well, why didn't you come into the station and ask?"

"Because I know you wouldn't tell me."

She sighed. "There are certain things we cannot disclose for fear of harming the investigation, yes. But I am sure I could bring you up to date, where possible. You cannot hang about the car park like this, and you won't learn anything if you do. I hope you're not charging the families for this. If you are, I think they are due at least a partial refund." She barely held back a grin. The man really was ridiculous. "You cannot be a private eye, or run a business, without proper systems in place. And if you need to be covert, make a better fist of it." The grin won. "Come into the station. I'll get you a cuppa. I want to get to know the families better anyway, as it happens, and you could help me."

He straightened his back, puffing out his chest, eyes wide with surprise. "Oh right, thank you... Lead the way."

She took Owen through to a free interview room, Dewi having offered to brew the tea.

Owen sat. "It doesn't feel right, talking to you in here." He pulled a face, eyes travelling around the interview room at the sound-proofing, and the video camera in the opposite corner above. "I feel like a suspect."

"Did you kill the students?"

"No."

"Then you do not need to worry."

He shifted in his seat. "Not everyone who hangs around an investigation is the culprit." He scowled. "I have a job to do."

Yvonne, sitting opposite, regarded him over the rim of her glasses. "So do I."

"Yeah, well, those families deserve to have answers, and they are not happy with how the investigation has proceeded so far. They think their voices have not been heard."

She sighed. "I am truly sorry the relatives feel like that. I can say is that the evidence has been gathered, examined, and preserved as it would have been were these deaths confirmed as murder from the start. Nothing has been lost. We had to be sure they were crimes before announcing as much to the families and the wider community. It would have been wrong to do otherwise, and could have resulted in fear where none was warranted. That sort of thing has knock-on effects for local businesses, and scares people who simply want to go out and enjoy themselves over Christmas. Surely, you can see that? We tread a fine line in this job."

"You said you wanted my help?" He leaned back in his chair.

A knock on the door signalled Dewi's arrival with the tea.

"I do." The DI rose to open the door. "But hanging around the station the way you are is making me look twice at you. Ian Huntley springs to mind."

"What?" He folded his arms, frowning. "Perhaps you don't need my help after all."

She passed him a steaming mug. "That should warm you up after your antics outside."

"You think this is funny?" He glowered at her. "What if I tell the families?"

She fixed him with a level gaze, her voice firm and direct. "I can assure you, I do not consider losing three young people in as many weeks a laughing matter. You can tell the families what you like, but no-one wants this killer caught more than my team and I."

"So, how can I help?" He frowned.

"You have spoken to all three families. Am I right?"

"Yes."

"Are they holding anything back? Something, perhaps,

they dare not tell us? Maybe, something their kids were mixed up in, that the parents are reluctant to give away because they are worried about consequences?"

"You mean like drugs or something?"

"Yes, anything along those lines. We know drug gangs have been infiltrating and working in the area. We've caught several. I do not think these youngsters were affiliated with gangs, but had they purchased anything from them? Had they interacted with anyone connected to gangs since coming home? I have a feeling something is being held back from us, and I don't know what that is. Have you heard anything that you think we should know? Obviously, I cannot make you tell us. But, if we are to stop further deaths, we need to know what the connection is. And if you have relevant information, and withhold it from us, you could be viewed by the courts as obstructing justice."

He shook his head. "They haven't told me anything that makes me think the deaths are connected. They are as much at a loss to explain what happened as we are, and they just want these crimes solved."

"Would you tell us if you heard anything that connected these murders?"

"Of course." His affirmation was emphatic. "I am being paid an hourly rate. I will get paid whatever the outcome, and if my information helped catch the killer? That could surely only help my reputation — which I am still trying to build, by the way."

"Good, I just wanted to be clear about that. If you learn anything which could aid us in catching this killer, I want to know about it as soon as you do."

"Got it." He unfolded his arms. "Thank you for the tea."

As she climbed the stairs back to CID, the DI wondered

whether she had just made a pact with the devil. They needed to keep their eye on Tim Owen.

THAT EVENING AFTER EATING, Yvonne settled back on cushions in front of a roaring fire in cotton pyjamas, with a glass of her favourite chardonnay.

Tasha joined her with a glass of red. "You are miles away... Do you want to talk about it?"

The DI gave her partner a wistful smile. "I'm enjoying having a little downtime with you. It's been a long couple of weeks, Tasha. I am so glad you are on leave until the New Year. It will be a luxury, having almost three uninterrupted weeks with you before you have to head back to London."

The psychologist hugged her. "I'm elated about it too, but I sense there is something else taking up your head-space. I'm here, if you need my help."

"I was hoping not to involve you in my work during your Christmas break, but we are currently working on a very troubling and puzzling case."

Tasha shrugged. "Well, run it past me here and now, while we are enjoying this glass of wine by the fire. I'll see what I can make of it. If you're not too tired?"

Yvonne related the case to her partner, going through each of the deaths and the jars found with each of the bodies.

Tasha pursed her lips, thinking, her gaze on the dancing flames of the fire. "I agree with you," she said, finally. "The jar is his signature, and I agree it must have meaning. The obvious takeaway is that the layers of onion equate to the layers of his story. He wants the world to know that tale, and he wants to punish someone or several someones."

"Go on..."

"But it isn't the kids. They were pawns to him. He has killed his victims without laying a finger on them. These are not up-close-and-personal murders. These are very much hands-off. That tells me he is likely punishing someone other than his victims. Probably, the people who care about the victims. Family and friends are the obvious targets here. I agree, it could be aimed at the local community, but then why choose youngsters who were usually living away? The community at large, although affected by the deaths, might arguably be less so than if the kids were living full time within the town."

"So you think he is aiming at friends and family?"

"I think that most likely, yes." Tasha nodded. "And I would go further... I think he is filled with remorse after each killing. Something happened to him or to someone he loved. If it were not for that, perhaps he might never have killed at all. Hence the hands-off approach. The deaths are a means to an end. And that end, and the story behind what he is doing, is the core of that onion. I also agree that the used matches represent the lives lost."

"Who are we looking for? What's his demographic?"

"I think he's young, possibly twenty-five to thirty-five years old. These are likely his first kills. But he has thought them through for some time, possibly years, before carrying them out. Perhaps he spent his teenage years ruminating about it. It will relate to pain in his past, or some perceived wrong-doing. I would talk to the parents again. Is there someone of around the same age as their dead loved ones who might bear a grudge? If anyone would know, they would. Explain that you think the grudge is likely against them or, less likely, against their children. Pick their brains. See what they say. Come back to me if that yields nothing.

Whoever your killer is, he evidently had time to plan in depth. He is a deep thinker and prefers spending time alone, but has a deep bond with his parents or parent. Thus he knows how much pain the victims' families will suffer."

"That is really helpful, Tasha, and reinforced the direction my own thoughts were taking. Do you think he will kill again?"

"Yes, if you do not find the answers, he will kill again. He isn't finished, and he won't be until you crack the case wide open and uncover his story. He doesn't care what happens to him in the end, but he cares his story is known in its entirety. I believe he needs someone to expose every part of whatever pains him. Only that will satisfy him. He will continue to kill everyone connected until you have the full story, or you have stopped him. But, be careful. I think he will kill himself once his tale is told. He will have achieved his aims, but the personal toll of his kills, and the pain he feels inside, will ultimately lead to his attempting suicide. It is possible he will try to take others with him, and that would include any police officers who try to stop him from taking his own life."

"Wow, that is an impressive profile, Tasha. No wonder the Met have hung on to you all these years." She smiled, sipping her wine. "I am in awe, and once again in your debt."

The psychologist slipped her arm around her partner, watching the fire. "You're welcome. I will get it all down on paper for you in the morning."

14

SOMETHING TO HIDE

"We told you our daughter was murdered." Mike Bevan stood outside his home, puffing his chest out, hands on hips. "You wouldn't listen, and now here we are."

Yvonne pressed her lips together, carefully choosing her words. "We are treating your daughter's death as murder, but we have yet to understand why Jacky was killed. And the motive will be crucial in finding her killer."

"It's all they talk about in town now. Everyone is scared. Some people won't let their kids out."

She nodded. "That is understandable."

"And you still haven't found the killer."

"May we come in?" she asked, a shiver travelling the length of her. It was bitter on the doorstep. She heard Dewi blowing on his hands behind.

Bevan reluctantly opened the door wide before leading them down the hall to the lounge.

The DI looked around for his wife, who was nowhere to be seen.

"Mandy is in bed," he explained, as though reading her thoughts.

"I see."

"She had a terrible night." He sighed. "Please, take a seat."

They did as they were told, Yvonne sitting on the sofa while Dewi chose one of the well-worn, brown leather armchairs.

The DI placed her bag on the carpet next to her feet. "You are correct, we haven't found the killer as yet."

He flicked his head as though to say, 'obviously.'

"But we are following up leads, and have a basic psychological profile of the perpetrator."

His eyes widened in surprise.

Yvonne continued. "We think he may be connected to you."

"To me?" Bevan frowned. "What do you mean? Connected how?"

"We believe he is someone who knows the families of all the victims, including your daughter. We think he is killing as revenge against the families or, perhaps, the friends."

"God, I hadn't thought of that." Mike ran a hand through his hair.

"Why would someone want to hurt your family? Have you any idea? Is there someone from your past that might bear a grudge?"

Bevan's eyes dropped to the carpet. They flicked from side to side as he considered it.

"We think the perpetrator might be young, if that helps? He may be a similar age to your daughter, or perhaps slightly older."

Mike swallowed, bringing his eyes back to the DI. "No."

"Oh..." Yvonne felt he answered too quickly. "Are you sure?"

"Yes."

"You don't have any suspicions? No-one in your past that could have a serious grudge?"

"No."

The DI watched him chew the inside of his cheek. "Would you tell us if you did?"

He frowned. "I want my daughter's killer found. Whatever it takes."

"Do you have any additional information for me at all?" She cocked her head. "Have any business deals gone awry? Or some other tragedy in your family's past?"

"Nope." He jutted out his chin.

"All right, well, think about it. If anything comes to mind over the next few days, get in touch. You have my number?"

"We do."

∾

YVONNE WAS DEFLATED as they left the Bevans' home. She turned to Dewi. "If it were my daughter, I would wrack my brains to help the inquiry. He closed down, like he is keeping something back."

Dewi nodded. "I agree. He is holding back. Something sprang to his mind, but whatever it was, he didn't want to disclose it. Let him mull things over. Perhaps he'll change his mind when he's had time to think about it."

"He'd better." The DI opened her car door. "He has a son to protect."

∾

THE SUN BROKE through the clouds as they pulled up outside of Bob and Diane Evans' house in Cambrian Gardens.

The DI straightened her coat and skirt on the way down the garden path, a familiar lump developing in her throat. It was difficult at the best of times, talking to the families of victims. But, having not yet identified a concrete suspect in their son's murder, this second visit to the family would be hard.

Dewi knocked on the double-glazed front door.

Bob and Diane Evans welcomed them into their living room, faces gaunt with grief.

The DI took a deep breath, trying her best to appear calm and composed. She didn't want them to close off to her, as Mike Bevan had done.

"Thank you for seeing us again," Dewi said, sitting opposite the couple. "We're doing everything we can to find out who killed Bryn."

Bob looked up with tired eyes. "It's been almost a month now. We still know nothing, not even how he came to be in that bin."

Yvonne nodded. "We understand how hard this is. But we are following up on several leads, and going over all the evidence, and we hoped you might help us."

Diane tilted her head, her voice quivering with emotion. "Help you, how?"

The DI hesitated for a moment before answering. "We think the killer may have a connection to you, and to the families of the other two victims."

Bob and Diane exchanged a look of confusion. "What connection?" asked Bob.

"We're not sure," Dewi answered. "But we believe the killer targeted your son, along with the other victims, for a specific reason. We're hoping you might help us identify the motive."

Diane rubbed her forehead, trying to think. "We don't know of anyone who would want to harm our son."

"Did he have enemies?" asked Yvonne.

Bob shook his head. "Not that we know of. He was a good lad, never got into trouble."

Dewi leaned forward. "What about any ex-partners or acquaintances? Anyone who might have held a grudge?"

Diane thought for a moment. "There was a girl he dated a few years ago, but they ended things amicably. And he has been living away while at university. I don't see why anyone from college would come all the way here to hurt him."

"The connection may be related to you as a family." Yvonne rubbed her chin. "And it could be historical. Perhaps, even, something you had put to the back of your minds long ago."

There was a flicker in Diane's eyes, barely perceptible, but it flared nonetheless. "I can't think of anything," she said, colour rising in her cheeks. She put her hands to her face, turning to her husband. "Can you, Robert?"

His forehead creased as he puzzled over it. "No, I can't." He shrugged. "I'm sorry."

The DI leaned back in her chair; her gaze never leaving the couple. She wanted to push Diane harder. The mother was hiding something. "Are you sure there's nothing you can think of?" she asked, her voice gentle but firm.

Diane shook her head, eyes still hidden behind her hands. "I'm sorry. I really can't think of anything."

Bob shifted in his seat, his expression pained. "We just want justice for our son. We want whoever did this caught and punished."

Dewi nodded. "We want that too. And we're doing everything in our power to make that happen. But we need your help, Mr and Mrs Evans. If you remember anything, anything at all, please call us."

The couple nodded, their shoulders slumped with exhaustion and grief.

Yvonne and Dewi rose to leave, Dewi pausing at the door to look back at the couple. "Please think carefully about this. Not only do we need to catch your son's killer, but we have to stop this murderer before another youngster dies. So call us... please?"

THEIR FINAL DESTINATION that day was the picturesque village of Bettws, the home of Tom and Mary Jarvis.

Picturesque villages, the DI mused, quaint places in idyllic settings, filled with tidy houses and tidy people; havens of peace, safety, and tranquillity. That was Bettws until now. The village was certainly tidy and peaceful, but with a hint of something else these days: a discordant hum, as if the rhythm of the bubbling brook itself had been disturbed. Words, of course, have their own life and can lie, but it was at precisely this point, when quiet life faltered and meaning slipped, when the soot from the fireplace stung the eyes, or the pilot light refused to burn, that truth could bring about solace, and the hope of resolution. It was surely the time when the parents of the murdered youngsters should tell them everything they knew.

Having so far failed to find the connection between the other victims' families and the killer, they hoped that Carl's parents would be more forthcoming.

The Jarvises welcomed the detectives with a mixture of curiosity and apprehension. They knew why the detectives were there, but appeared at a loss for how they could help, still reeling from the shock of their son's loss.

As they sat in the living room, sipping tea, the detectives probed them with gentle questions. "Did Carl have any enemies? Was he involved in illegal activities?"

Tom shook his head. "Carl was a quiet, hardworking boy who loved studying, playing the guitar, and writing his own songs. He didn't mix with the wrong crowd, and he had a keen sense of right and wrong. We brought him up that way."

"Can you think of anyone from your past who might want to hurt you using the death of your son as a weapon?" Yvonne scrutinised both parents. "Perhaps something happened in the past that left someone outraged or disgruntled enough to want to cause your family harm? Maybe somebody with poor mental health?" She was clutching at straws, looking for anything that might jog a memory.

Tom fell silent, hands on his knees; head bowed.

Mary spoke for him. "I can't think of anyone we know who is like that. We've led a quiet life. We're not socialites. The business takes up a lot of our time and, even before we started it, we were always working."

"And there were no problems with work?"

"None that would have been that serious, no."

Yvonne scribbled notes, glancing up at Tom now and then. He seemed uneasy, and the DI couldn't shake the feeling there was something he wanted to say. She leaned forward in her chair, placing a hand on his arm. "Tom, is there something you're not telling us?"

He looked up, his eyes meeting hers. For a moment, Yvonne saw something spark behind them, but it was gone before she could grasp it.

"Nothing important," he replied, his voice unsteady.

She wasn't convinced, but knew pressing him might make him clam up further. Instead, she turned to Mary. "Do you really not know who might have done this to your son?"

Mary shook her head, tears pooling in her eyes. "I can't imagine who would do this. We've had no enemies, and have never caused trouble."

Yvonne gave her a nod. "Very well... I am sorry to have quizzed you like this."

"You think this person knows us?" Tom rubbed his forehead.

"We believe it is possible. But, unless you can think of how they might know you, it isn't something that will help us. We want you to ponder it, and get in touch if you remember anything that could be relevant."

"I'll see you out." Tom rose from his chair, his face a mask.

The DI resisted the urge to tell him she knew he was hiding something. Perhaps now wasn't the time, but something about this case just didn't add up. Something more lurked beneath the surface. Whatever languished there, Yvonne was determined to find it, with or without their cooperation.

15

DISASTER STRIKES

He hid in the shadows, one hand on the rag in his pocket, scared his thumping heart and anxious breathing would be heard.

A multitude of stars littered the sky. They blurred in the mist of breath as he exhaled. The night air was crisp; a deep frost developing on the hedgerow.

Footsteps approached, an uneven tapping on the tarmac, the ragged rhythm of a man who'd been drinking.

The predator waited. It wouldn't do to jump out too soon. If his target took flight, there were no guarantees he would catch up with him. Timing was critical.

He took a deep breath.

Now.

He stepped out from under the hedge.

"What the-" His victim's next words were smothered by the rag, the target becoming limp after only a few seconds.

He pulled a malleable arm around his shoulders, half-carrying; half-dragging the unconscious man. If they were seen by anyone, he would shrug it off. Just a drunken friend who needed help to get home. But he didn't want spectators. It would mean

calling off his plan. And that wouldn't do, not when his story was
so close to concluding.

FRANCES HOWELLS' polo shirt was coming out of her
trousers, her hair stuck out at odd angles, and her face
appeared puffy and tear-soaked as she slammed open the
doors to the station.

Yvonne stopped in her tracks, a file tucked under her
arm. "Mrs Howells? What's the matter? What's happened?"

Frances held up an unlabelled jar. "My son is missing,
and this was left on my doorstep. I don't know who left it, or
why, but my son did not return to his house after leaving his
friends at the pub last night."

The DI ran a hand through her hair. "Right, you'd better
give me that, and come in and tell us everything you know."
She led the distressed mother to an interview room. "Please
wait here while I find DS Hughes. We will bag this jar in
case it is needed as evidence, and we will be with you in just
a few minutes. We'll put out an alert for your son as soon as
we have the details from you."

Yvonne rushed to CID to find her team, grabbing a
plastic evidence bag on the way. She held it up as soon as
she joined the others. "Tony Howells is missing, and his
mother found this on her doorstep. It is an unlabelled jar
containing an onion core and an unlit match."

"Unlit?" Dewi frowned.

"Yes, as in not used," the DI confirmed. "I don't know
where Tony is, but I think he may still be alive. I think that is
the significance of the unburned match."

She bagged the jar, giving it an evidence tag. "Dewi, can
you come with me? We'll get everything we can from

Frances. Dai, could you or Callum get this to forensics, please? And, could you delve into Tony Howells' social media immediately? We will call you with more information as soon as we have it. You can put out an alert out to all units as soon as I have phoned you with the details."

"Will do, ma'am." Dai nodded.

The DI and Dewi left to rejoin Frances.

"This is different, isn't it?" The DS puffed as they ran down the flight of stairs. "The jars are usually left with a body."

"Perhaps something has changed... We'll need time to think this through, but it looks like Tony may be alive somewhere. The question is: was he responsible for leaving that jar on his mother's doorstep?"

"You think her son could be the killer?"

"I think we should explore that possibility."

They paused at the door of the interview room.

Yvonne added in hushed tones, "Remember, Frances does not know the significance of these jars. We shouldn't reveal too much about them, but I would like to know why an abductor would leave it where he did? Tony does not live with his mum. So, either he is the murderer, or the killer had prior knowledge of the family and where they live."

"Let's find out what she knows." Dewi pushed the interview room door open.

"Mrs Howells?" Yvonne sat across the desk from her interviewee.

Dewi sat next to the DI.

"Have you started looking for my son?" Frances looked from one to the other, her red eyes underscored by shadows.

"We've set things in motion." Yvonne leaned in. "But we need more information from you."

"I'll tell you everything I can." She pulled a hanky from her pocket and blew her nose.

"Where did your son go last night?"

"He was at the Exchange Bar on Back Lane."

"When did he leave the bar? And when was the last time you heard from him?"

"He left shortly after midnight to walk home. He lives on Plantation Lane. I didn't hear from him this morning. He is on holiday from work for Christmas, and he was due to meet me for coffee, shopping, and lunch. When he didn't show, I phoned him. His mobile phone is dead and his home phone went straight to the answerphone. I texted his best friend, who said that they had last seen him at midnight. That's when I went out in the car park at the back of the shop to check for any sign of him, and found this jar on the doorstep. It's probably just someone's trash, but I brought it here in case it is connected. I thought it was odd that someone would leave it there."

"You did the right thing, Frances." Yvonne nodded. "We'll check with all the officers who were in town last night and go through CCTV. In the meantime, if he gets in touch, I want you to let us know immediately."

"Am I right to be worried? I mean, it's not like him to go dark like this. Tony is always in touch. He knows I worry. He usually lets me know he is okay, and he didn't last night. I expected a text to say he was home safe, but there was nothing. He has forgotten once or twice before, so I wasn't overly worried until he didn't show at ten this morning. I tried contacting him at ten-fifteen, and then again at ten-thirty, and nothing. By eleven, I was seriously worried. That's when I went out to check the carpark at the back of the shop, and found the jar. I saw one in the dumpster the day I found the body. I had forgotten about it until finding this one. Does it mean my Tony is dead?" She wiped a tear from her cheek with the back of her hand.

Yvonne flicked a glance at Dewi before answering. "You must stay positive, Frances. We have nothing to suggest that anything bad has happened to your son. The jar in the bin accompanied a body. The one you found today did not. We will do everything in our power to find Tony. Could you give me a name and contact number for his best friend? We'll need a description of the clothes he was wearing, so we can put out an alert, and find him on CCTV. We will also ping his phone."

"His best friend is Craig Miles." Frances fished her mobile out of her jacket pocket and flicked through the contents. "This is his number." She held the phone out so the detectives could note it down. "Would you like me to call him now?" she asked.

The DI nodded. "We would appreciate it if you could. It would save time. I'd like to speak to him, if I may?"

Frances tapped in the number. "I'll say hello and then hand it over to you."

Yvonne accepted the phone from Tony's mother, after Frances had explained to Tony's friend what was happening. "Hello?"

"This is Craig." His voice shook and cracked. He was clearly hungover.

"I am DI Yvonne Giles, Craig. I'd like you to tell me what happened last night. Where is Tony?"

"I dunno..." He sighed. "We all agreed to share a taxi home and booked an SUV. It's cheaper that way. But, you know, Tony's been working out. He has his fitness regime, and he wanted to walk. He doesn't get drunk that often. And, when he does, he walks home unless he is completely legless. Well, last night, he wasn't legless. But he had quite a few pints and was drunk. He said he could walk home and wanted the fresh air as it helps him sleep."

"What time did he leave you?"

"He was the first to leave, around midnight. Our taxi came about ten-past. Most of us were working this morning at the factory. That's why we didn't stay out later. We would usually stay out until two or three in the morning, but three of us had to work. Tony wasn't due in the factory today. He had started his Christmas leave. We start ours tomorrow."

"Did you hear from him after he left you? I mean, did you text him? Did he text you?"

"No, I didn't hear from him. But that isn't unusual. We don't normally text each other after leaving the pub. And most of us were going to see each other today, anyway. I wish I had told him to text me to say he got home safe. But, I didn't. I didn't know there was a problem until his mum rang me at work."

"What was he wearing last night?"

"He had on a blue-check cotton shirt, and blue jeans. I don't remember what he was wearing on his feet. But we have photos of him on our phone. We can let you have those if you like?"

"That would be good. We will put out an alert with a description now, but we will need the photos for news bulletins and posters if he is not found."

"No problem."

"Has anyone been to his home?"

"Only his mum."

"One moment..." The DI put her hand over the mobile. "Frances, did you go inside your son's house?"

Mrs Howells shook her head. "No, I don't have a key. I rang the doorbell and peered through the downstairs windows. There was no sign of him."

Yvonne spoke into the phone again. "Craig, if you hear from Tony, please let us know straight away. You can reach me on the following." She gave him her mobile number. "You can also text me the photos you have of him."

"I'll text you those straight after this call," he agreed.

16

MISSING

Tony Howells' home on Plantation Lane was less than fifteen minutes' drive from the station.

They parked on the main road, two doors down, and made their way through the small wooden gate, accompanied by two constables who would bash the door open if needed.

Although the grass was trimmed, he had spent little time in the garden. There were no flowers or shrubs, only a small patch of grass bounded by box hedging, and a straight concrete-paved path which led to the doorstep.

Dewi rang the bell, and they hung back, holding their breath, listening for any sign of someone inside. "Police, open up!"

Again they waited.

The DS shook his head. "It doesn't look like he's here."

Yvonne nodded. "Let's go in."

They stood back, allowing the burly PCs to swing their battering ram at the door.

It gave way on the second heave.

The uniformed officers led the sweep, while Yvonne and

Dewi called out to Tony. There was no answer. He wasn't home.

Yvonne found his bedroom on the second floor.

The bed had been roughly made, and two discarded shirts and a pair of trousers lay on top. A faint whiff of cologne hung in the air.

The wardrobe doors were wide open, exposing the clothing inside. The red velvet curtains were closed.

"I don't believe he came home." Yvonne grimaced. "He's still out there."

A commotion outside drew Dewi to the window. "Frances is here," he announced. "She's arguing with the officers on the door, and wants to come in."

"I'll go talk to her." Yvonne left the room, taking the stairs down to where the anxious mum stood on the step, hands on hips.

"He's my son. I have a right to see what's happening for myself."

"Please, Frances, I understand you are worried, but we have a job to do." She took the frightened mum by the elbow. "I need your help."

"What is it?" Frances asked, wide-eyed.

"Does your son drive a vehicle? And, if he does, do you see it here?"

The woman surveyed parked vehicles up and down the road. "Yes, there it is..." She pointed to a silver Audi, parked one hundred yards away. "That is my son's car."

Yvonne narrowed her eyes. "Thank you."

"He's not here, is he?" Frances' eyes filled with tears.

"He isn't, but we have officers examining CCTV and pinging his phone. We should have a location soon."

The frightened woman pulled at her hair with her

hands. "We should check the bins on the way here in case... in case..."

"We have officers doing that too." Yvonne pressed her lips together.

"There was nothing in mine. It was the first place I... Oh, God." Frances pressed a hand to her stomach, as though about to vomit into the hedge.

The DI walked over to support her, but the woman straightened up. "I'd better telephone his father."

"His father?" Yvonne frowned. "Where is he?"

Frances gave a dismissive wave. "Oh, he doesn't live around here. He moved to Jersey several years ago. Jeff's holed up there with some young thing he met nine years ago. But he loves his son, and he would want to know what is happening."

"I see." The DI nodded. "I don't have any objections to you calling him. Listen, I'd better get on, Frances. I'm afraid you cannot go into the house just yet. We don't know if it is a crime scene, and my DS is searching for anything which might help us with your son's location. I suggest you go home for now. If your son gets in touch, please let us know immediately."

"Will you call me if you find him?" Mrs Howells wiped her cheek with her sleeve. "Don't keep me waiting if you know something."

Yvonne nodded. "I will call you."

CALLUM GREETED them when they got back to CID. "Someone cut the cables to the CCTV cameras on New Road. Two cables cut in all. Engineers are repairing them as we speak, and installing metal protectors to prevent it happening again. It will be another twenty-four hours, at least, before they are operational."

Yvonne frowned. "Do we have footage from before they were cut? Have we got the perpetrator on camera?"

"We have, but whoever did it was clearly savvy. They kept themselves out of frame for most of it. Camera operators didn't pick the perp up. I think he must have approached from behind the cameras. He comes into a frame for less than a second, wearing dark clothing, probably black, and a face mask. His eyes are visible, but it's night, and I doubt he is recognisable from what we have. Sorry to be the bearer of bad news."

"Could you take a still image of him to Frances Howells, please? She's gone back to her shop. Ask her if she recognises the person in the photo."

"Do you think this could be Tony?" he asked.

"It's possible. I'm keeping an open mind. We could not rule him out, and something has changed. The jar his mother found contained an unused match and the onion core, which suggests Tony is alive, and his disappearance relates to the heart of the story — whatever it is he wants the world to know. If the perp is Tony Howells, his mother would be the most likely person to recognise him on the CCTV. Also, she's keen to know we are doing something. It will help put her mind at rest on that score."

"On it..." Callum nodded. "I'll call you after I have spoken to her."

Dai approached with three mugs of coffee. "I thought you would appreciate this. You haven't stopped yet today."

"Thank you," the DI took hers, followed by Dewi.

"Thanks, Dai." Dewi took a sip. "Have you got a location for Tony Howells's phone yet?"

The DC grimaced. "Not yet, but we're working on it. We

have data from two cell towers, and waiting on a third. Once we have that, we should be able to triangulate to within a few miles. Otherwise, we have a thirty-mile radius to deal with. I think the phone is somewhere north of Newtown, but we'll need to tighten up the location."

"He doesn't have GPS on his phone?"

"Not as far as I can tell. We've got no reading for him, but he could be in a blind spot. I can't rule that out. I only know we haven't got a signal."

"Good work, Dai, keep on it." Yvonne smiled. "And thank you for the coffee."

17

BOMBSHELL

They hadn't finished their coffee before Callum was back, panting from running upstairs. "Frances Howells is in reception, ma'am. She's in a bit of a state and keeps saying it is all her fault. She's repeating the same phrase over and over. I think you should try speaking to her. I couldn't make any sense of it."

"Right, no problem. I'll get down there now."

TEARS STREAMED DOWN the mother's face as the DI led her to an interview room and asked a PC to bring a cup of tea for the sobbing woman.

"Here, take a seat." Yvonne pulled out a chair and guided her into it. "Now then, take a deep breath for me, and tell me what has upset you. Has Tony turned up?"

"N-no." She shook her head. "Th-there's something I have to tell you." Frances let out a sob, spittle forming strands between her lips. "I should have told you before, I just... I wasn't sure. I'm still not... But..."

"Take your time." The DI's voice was soft. "Take another breath."

"This is about Helen Turner," Frances said finally.

"Helen Turner? Who is Helen Turner?"

"The woman who died."

"I don't understand." Yvonne scratched her head. "When did she die, and who are we talking about? This is a new name for me."

"She was our friend. She died in the winter of nineteen-ninety-eight, after a night out. It shouldn't have happened. We were young and full of it. We were having a wild night: drinking and experimenting with drugs. It got crazy. It got out of hand, and Helen... I'd better start from the beginning," Frances said finally.

"I'm listening." The DI pulled out a chair for herself, sitting next to the woman.

"We had gone to a party in Argae Hall. It closed down years ago but, back then, it was a place we went to dance, and drink, and have a good time. Our friend Mike was driving, and there were five of us altogether: myself, Mike, Helen, Diane, and Tom. We hadn't been out together for a while. We had been friends since school, but some of us had been away at college, and we hadn't gone out together in nearly a year."

"Go on..."

"Well, it was early December, and college had broken up for Christmas. Like I said, we got together after months of not seeing each other. There was an event on at Argae Hall. We danced, drank alcohol, and had a great time. But Mike, our designated driver, couldn't enjoy himself like the rest of us. We were sad that he couldn't drink. So we worked on him, persuading him to drink alcohol and let his hair down. He stood firm, to begin with, but later on he gave in and started drinking. We were not thinking of how we were going to get home. In the back of my mind, I had this vague notion we could get a taxi and it would all be fine. And we carried on drinking. Mike got merry. He wasn't as drunk as the rest of us. I mean, he'd had a few pints by the end of the night, but he wasn't loud like we were becoming. Tom had brought cannabis with him. We wouldn't have dared do it inside the venue, but we puffed it outside. I had LSD in my handbag. I knew it was wrong, and I had only tried it once before. Someone at college had offered me a few tabs to go home with and try over Christmas, so I took them. I don't know what was I thinking. I know it was wrong, experimenting like that..."

"Were you using LSD that night?"

"Not right away, no. And, to be honest, I was in two minds. I had it in my purse, but I wasn't sure we should do anything with it, and I almost threw it away. I wish I had. But I didn't. We couldn't get a taxi home. Everything was booked up. The taxi firms all said we should have booked in advance because Christmas is always busy and booked up. So, we were stuffed."

"And Mike drove?" Yvonne cocked her head.

"Yeah, he did. We used the back roads, heading towards Montgomery, and turned off towards Sarn and Kerry. And it was while we were in the back of the car that I offered a tab to Helen. She hadn't used the drug before, and I had only tried it once. I wasn't expecting what happened next."

"Did you have a bad trip?"

"I didn't, but Helen did."

"Go on..."

"Her eyes were wild, and she became afraid and angry all at the same time. She flailed her arms about and was banging on the car door and screaming, wanting to be let out. We were passed by a police car, and we were terrified. Mike panicked, because he had been drinking, and the rest of us were heavily intoxicated. He was scared the police would come back. He pulled over in the country lane and let her out. Next thing we knew, she had disappeared through a metal gate into a field, and carried on running. It was like she was possessed. We wanted to go after her, but Mike wouldn't let us. He really was petrified the police would come back and catch us. So we got back into the car and continued on to Newtown. We thought she would be taken in by a farmhouse. It was freezing outside. The fields were already white with frost, but we honestly thought she would be taken in."

"And she wasn't?"

"That's right, she wasn't. I woke up at mid-day, and Diane called to tell me Helen was missing. No-one knew where she was, and her partner and parents were frantic. Later that day, a farmhand found her body in a barn. They said she died of hypothermia, and they had found drugs and alcohol in her system. The police talked to us, wanting to know how she ended up where she did. We lied and denied knowing anything about it. We stuck to our story that we dropped her off at the top of town and, although they suspected we were lying, they had no proof. And the autopsy concluded she died of hypothermia, hastened by her level of intoxication. There was nothing more to be done. The case was closed."

"She left the car because she was having a bad LSD trip?"

Frances nodded, lowering her head. "I feel awful. I have felt terrible since that day whenever I remember what we did."

"Do you think those events are linked to what is

happening today?" Yvonne put a hand on the woman's shoulder, bringing her back to the present. "Frances? Do you think someone is exacting revenge for Helen's death?"

The woman's head snapped up, her eyes wide. "All the dead youngsters are our children. Everyone else who was in the car with Helen has lost a child. You can't let this happen to my son."

"Do you know who is doing this?"

"I think it is Helen's son, Peter."

"Peter Turner!" The DI put a hand to her head. "The courier... He is Helen's son."

"Yes, Peter Turner is Helen Turner's son. He was twelve months old when she died, and was looked after at home by his father. Peter couldn't remember his mum. He was too young. I felt terrible watching him grow up without her, knowing I was at least partly responsible for her death. So I grew close to the boy. I encouraged him to my shop and gave him free food. I was still doing that now whenever he was home. And two years ago, I told him everything — confessed it all."

"How did he respond?"

"He was quiet, not saying very much. It affected him I could tell, but he seemed to brush it off and the next time I saw him, he was the same old Peter. I was so relieved. It felt like a massive weight had slipped from my shoulders, a weight I had carried around all those years. Only now I believe he is punishing us. I am terrified for my boy. You must find him. I honestly didn't think Peter would take my son. I told him how sorry and devastated I was about his mum's loss, and explained that the others felt the same way. Now I realise I messed up all over again, trying to do the right thing."

The DI called her team, telling them to look for Peter

Turner and his van, before turning her attention back to Frances. "You realise that I have to report the information you have given me? We will do everything in our power to find Turner and get your son back alive. But you must also know you have informed me about a historical crime. And that I will have to pass that information on to an investigation team."

Frances nodded, tears falling from her cheeks.

"I am so sorry that you are going through this, and that you learned these lessons the way you did. I am sure there are people out there who have done similar things and never suffered the loss of a friend. But you have done the right thing by telling us now, and it may help get your son back safe. I must leave you, but I will ask an officer to help you get your things together and get home."

"Am I free to go?" she asked.

"You are... We will keep you informed of our progress. In the weeks to come, you may wish to consult with a solicitor, as Helen's case will probably be reopened. But right now, your focus should rightly be on Tony."

"Thank you." Frances took out a hanky and wiped her face. She turned her red eyes to the detective. "Please call me the minute you know anything?"

Yvonne nodded. "We will."

THE EXCITEMENT WAS PALPABLE. Five young people, their whole lives ahead of them, were out in the world and getting theirs.

"Pass it over." Helen reached for the spliff. "Come on, you've had more than your fair share."

"You need one of these." Frances pulled a small square of paper from her purse. "Put it on your tongue."

"Are you sure that's a good idea?" Mike, driving, asked. "Helen hasn't tried it before. What if it goes bad?"

"Oh, shut up and drive." Helen laughed. "Don't worry so much," she said, placing the paper in her mouth.

Barely moments later, she was desperate to get out of the car; attacking anyone who tried to stop her.

∿

HER BREATH CAME IN SHORT, laboured bursts as the cold air stung her face and pained her lungs. She would have given up, but this was no ordinary run. It was life or death; the girl forced her aching limbs onward.

Numbing cold gave way to heat as the chill penetrated deep into her skin, misleading the pain receptors within. She tossed her bag and jacket to the ground.

The monster was coming. A vile beast, hard on her heels, grunting and panting. So much noise.

He had followed her from the car, pounding the earth somewhere behind. Somewhere she dared not look.

As she tumbled into the frozen dirt, grit and stone scraped and penetrated the numbed the skin on her knees, hands, and cheek.

Still it came: the thump, thump, thump of feet. Bang, bang, bang in her ears as she lay on the ground panting for air.

The girl dragged herself up and sprinted on towards the light coming from a barn. At last, somewhere to hide.

She ripped off her blouse, tossing that too before reaching the shed door, heaving it open, and crouching inside.

Gradually her breathing slowed as an overwhelming urge to sleep replaced the fear.

Let the monster come. She no longer cared.

18

A CHILL WIND

Tony Howells woke from a sleep so deep his back and stomach ached from lying in the same position for hours.

It took several seconds for his clouded vision to clear, and for him to realise he was in the back of a van. Although his head and body hurt, he had not been restrained. He checked himself over and, as far as he could tell, he was uninjured.

"Hello?" he called. "Can anyone hear me?"

There was no reply.

He put an ear to the carpet lining the van's walls. "Hello? Can anyone hear me?"

He banged with his fist. Thump, thump, thump. "Hello? Let me out of here, do you hear me? Let me out."

Tony made his way to the back doors by feeling around the dark space. "Hello?" He pushed and kicked at them, to no avail. "Come on, it's cold in here."

Again, he put his ear to the door. Nothing.

He heard a clunk, followed by the whirring noise of a fan kicking into action. Cold air began flooding the room.

Dressed only in jeans, a cotton shirt, and a thin coat, Tony zipped up his jacket to protect himself from the chill on his neck and back.

The van's engine fired up, and the vehicle lurched forward with a crunching of gears.

Its captive hunkered on the floor, hugging his knees.

BACK IN THE INCIDENT ROOM, Dai attempted to triangulate the positions of both Tony Howells and Peter Turner's mobile phones.

Yvonne caught up with him. "How are we doing?"

"We've located them to within a twelve-mile radius. They are somewhere in the Elan Valley. The area is vast, as you know, and there are large bodies of water and forested areas. We've got mobile units out there looking, and a chopper from North Wales is on its way, so we'll have eyes in the skies. But it could be some time before we locate them. If he is parked up in a lay-by or on a road, we should find them faster but, if he's found cover, it could be longer."

Callum called over. "Turner's phone is ringing, but he isn't answering."

The DI pursed her lips. "Keep trying... If he has a signal, it may mean he is out in the open somewhere. As soon as we have a firm location, I'm heading out there."

"Not on your own, you're not." The DCI had approached from behind.

She jumped, swinging round, hand to her chest. "Can you not do that?"

"Sorry, I just don't want you chasing this madman on your own. I know what you're like, so I am keeping an eye on you."

"I won't be on my own." She raised an eyebrow. "Dewi will come with me, and we'll have uniformed officers as backup. An armed response unit and dog team are on standby, ready to go when we know where to send them."

"I'll be coming too," Llewelyn asserted. "Peter Turner may be responsible for three deaths already. I don't want him increasing his tally any further. We don't know if he is armed."

"I doubt he will be." Yvonne rubbed her chin. "It's not his style." She peered around at Llewelyn's back.

"What are you doing?" He frowned.

"Looking for your cape, sir." She grinned.

He pulled a face. "Hilarious... I am just making sure you don't take unnecessary risks."

TONY RUBBED HIS HEAD, trying to shake the thick, groggy feeling washing over him. Too warm, he unzipped his jacket and loosened the top buttons of his shirt. "Hello?" he called again. "Please talk to me... Let me out..." He didn't recognise his voice, or the way the words slurred — like his mouth could no longer articulate them properly.

His eyelids felt heavy as his jaw gaped in a yawn. He curled himself into the foetal position and closed his eyes.

"YVONNE?" Dai called above the chatter in the room.

She ran over. "Have they found them?"

"The helicopter pilot thinks they have spotted Turner's location. A car is on its way to verify the van plates."

"Where is he?"

"He's in a forested area near the Caban-Coch Reservoir, about a forty minutes' drive from here. I have the GPS co-ordinates for the location, assuming it is confirmed."

"I know Caban-Coch well," Dewi was at her side. "I can drive us there. It's a beautiful area, but it isn't the easiest terrain to get around if he has gone off the road. We might be better off taking one of the Land Rovers."

She nodded. "We'll do that."

Dai held out notepaper with the co-ordinates. "They've got him. The mobile unit has confirmed the plates. It's Peter Turner's van."

"Make sure those officers stay back. They are not to approach, but wait in place for everyone else to arrive." Yvonne grabbed her coat. "Dai, make sure the armed unit and dog team are on their way." She turned to the DCI. "Are you coming?"

"Let's go."

They headed out in convoy, lights and sirens blaring; weaving in and out of cars until the traffic thinned as they left the town behind.

Rolling hills on either side of the road paled into blues and purples in the distance, the landscape stunning in the winter sun. It could be summer, but for the chill in the air. Grazing sheep trundled on, their thick coats giving them immunity to the frost-bitten air.

Forty minutes was a long time when someone's life was on the line. The DI ran through many scenarios in her head, her stomach churning as she prepared herself for whatever lay ahead.

"We must be close, we're almost at Caban-Coch," Dewi said.

"Just a little further," Yvonne agreed, comparing co-ordinates.

"I can see a car ahead." He pulled in behind another police vehicle, switching off the engine. "I'll speak with those boys; find out what's happening."

Yvonne and the DCI climbed out of the Land Rover, following Dewi along the road.

Two uniformed officers got out of their vehicle and pointed towards the tree line further along the road. "He's in there."

Yvonne squinted. Shading her eyes from the winter sun, she could barely make out the back of a white van amongst the trees. She took out her mobile and punched in the number for Peter Turner's phone.

Although it rang, no-one answered.

More police vans arrived, parking along the road behind, and a sudden burst of barking accompanied the dog team's arrival.

She turned to the DCI. "Shall we go?"

He looked along the line of vehicles to satisfy himself that armed response and the incident team had arrived before giving her the nod.

They followed the road to where Peter's van had clearly mown down part of the wire fence in his haste to find shelter amongst the trees.

Yvonne tried his mobile again. They were now barely a hundred yards from where he was parked.

This time he answered, his voice clipped. "Yes?"

"Is that Peter?" she asked. "Peter Turner?"

"Who's asking?"

She cleared her throat. "My name is Yvonne Giles. I am with Dyfed-Powys police."

"I have nothing to say to you-"

"Wait," she interjected. "I believe you are holding

someone we are looking for. His name is Tony Howells. I would like to speak with him. Can you put him on?"

"You're probably too late." His voice was hard; cold.

"Can we come closer? We want to talk to you."

"I have nothing to say, except I am almost done."

As armed officers moved to positions amongst the trees surrounding the vehicle, the DI held up a hand, signalling them to wait. "Peter, I know about your mum. I know what happened, but this is not the way to bring her justice. She would not have wanted this."

"How would you know what my mum wanted? She never had the chance to want very much. Her future was taken away by her so-called friends; cowards too scared to tell the police where she was and why she was there."

"And they will have to answer for what happened that night. We are aware of it now. But harming people who had nothing whatever to do with your mum's death is not the answer. You know it isn't. Your mum would not have wanted that."

"I want it," he growled. "I want them punished for what they did."

"It's not right, harming the innocent to punish the guilty. We will investigate fully your mother's death, but we need you to release Tony now. He has been through enough."

Turner was silent.

"Peter, armed officers are surrounding your vehicle. You have nowhere to go. We will move in slowly, and I want you to remain calm. We want to end this with no one else being injured. Come out of your vehicle with your hands on your head. Can you do that for us?"

Yvonne and the DCI were now twenty feet from the driver's side of the van. They could clearly see Turner as he watched them approach.

Something glinted from inside the cab.

"He has a knife." Llewelyn halted in his tracks, his hand out towards the DI.

Turner held the blade to his jugular. "Don't come any closer," he yelled down the phone. "I'll end it here. I've got a combination lock on the back. If I die, Howells does too. You wouldn't get him out in time. It's minus eighteen back there. He won't last long."

Yvonne's heart pounded, her mind racing. She took a deep breath and spoke calmly into the phone. "Peter, listen to me. We don't want anyone else to get hurt. Let's talk about this. We can work this out."

"I've done all the talking I want to. I don't care. Do you hear me?" Turner spat back. "I'm not going to prison. I would rather die."

Yvonne felt sweat beading on her brow and the small of her back. The silence of the others was palpable, every officer holding their breath. She glanced over at the DCI, who gave a nod, a silent show of support.

"Peter, I understand you're angry, and you want justice for your mother. But hurting innocent people won't bring her back. It will only make matters worse," she continued, her voice as steady and even as she could make it.

Turner sneered. "You know nothing about losing someone like that. I was barely a year old. They took away my mother before I knew her, before I was even old enough to store the memories of the time I had with her. I cannot forgive them for that. And they were too miserable and cowardly to tell the police where she was. She died in that barn because they were afraid of getting into trouble and losing their precious college places. Pathetic... If they had flagged down the police and told them what happened, she would have been saved instead of taking hours to die in that barn. But they didn't. They left her there."

"Peter, I know it's hard," Yvonne said, her voice soft. "But harming the innocent will not change what happened or bring her back. It won't make the pain go away. Your mother wouldn't have wanted this for you. She was proud of you, her heart filled with love for her baby. She would not have wanted you to hurt her friends' sons and daughters for revenge. That is not how she would have brought you up."

Turner's grip on the knife tightened, his knuckles turning white. "I don't know what she would have wanted. I never got to know her."

"Then let us help you find out," Yvonne said. "We can investigate her death. We can find out what really happened. But we need you to put down the knife and come out of the van. You can still make your mother proud at this moment. You can let this go. It's what she would have wanted."

"Justice for my mother. That's all I want. It's all I've ever wanted."

"We can give you that," Yvonne said. "But we need you to put down the knife and come out of the van. We can sort this out together."

There was a long pause, Yvonne wiping her brow with her fingertips, breath clouding in the cold air. She pursed her lips, waiting for his response.

Finally, the knife fell away from Turner's neck, his head bowed and shoulders hunched. He looked like a man whose fight had left him.

They watched as he stepped out, his hands held up in surrender. Armed officers moved in, weapons trained on him as they searched for the knife. Yvonne approached slowly, her heart thudding in her chest. She could see the pain etched on Turner's face, the agony of loss still raw.

"I'm sorry for what happened to your mother," she said, her voice low. "I meant what I said. We can help you get the answers you seek, even while you yourself face justice. We can find out what really happened to your mum and those responsible will answer for it."

Turner looked up at her, his eyes red. "I wish I could believe you," he said, his voice barely a whisper.

"I keep my word." Yvonne answered. "But you have three deaths to answer for. Do not make it four. We need the combination for the lock on the van door. Let us get Tony Howells out alive."

He mumbled the numbers while the DI wrote them down. She relayed them to Dewi, who was at the back of the van.

The DS wrenched open the doors, clambering inside to the unconscious victim. As he worked hard to wake him up, the shirtless Tony Howells muttered incoherently before attempting to go back to sleep.

Two uniformed officers helped Dewi get Tony out of the van, where paramedics were waiting to revive him and checking his vital signs before whisking him off to the hospital in a waiting ambulance.

Yvonne prayed they had gotten to him in time.

19

THE TRUTH WILL OUT

Tony Howells lay like a cyborg in his hospital bed in Shrewsbury, tubes and wires linking him to various monitors and mechanical equipment, his eyes closed.

Frances sat at his bedside in the ITU, holding his hand and stroking the back of it with her thumb, careful not to disturb the cannula through which he received a drip. She didn't take her eyes from his face as she waited for him to wake.

Yvonne stood near the door when the nurse let her in, in two minds whether to disturb the attentive mother.

As though sensing someone was there, Frances turned to look. Her eyes widened when she saw the DI and, letting go of her son's hand, she rose from her seat to greet the detective. "You saved him. You saved my Tony." She grabbed Yvonne's arms. "Thank you. I thought we'd lost him, and I was so scared." She looked back at the bed. "He isn't completely out of the woods yet, but he is stable, and the doctors think he will be okay."

"I'm glad to hear it." Yvonne smiled. "And it was a team effort."

"Sorry?"

"The rescue... There were a lot of us in that field. Everyone played their part."

Frances nodded. "What has happened to Peter?"

Yvonne pressed her lips together. "It won't go to trial. He is pleading guilty to three counts of kidnapping and murder, and one count of attempted murder. He told the arresting officers he wants to be punished to the fullest extent of the law. Peter said he is a man who owns up to his responsibilities."

Frances lowered her eyes. "They've been in touch: Mike, Diane, and Tom."

"Do they know they could face charges?"

"Yes." She nodded. "They are ready. We all agree it is right. We should have come forward a long time ago. I hadn't seen or heard from them since that night. It was something not to be spoken about. We slinked off into our new lives. They and I have lived with this hanging over us all these years. There was never any peace, you know? She was always there. I saw her regularly before I went to sleep. Now it is out in the open, and a weight has lifted. I feel terrible for Peter, and for my friends' dead loved ones. I so wish that things had been different. That we had acted differently. Facing up to it now is the least I can do. If I had lost my son, well..."

Yvonne nodded. "I'm glad you didn't. And I wish you and Tony well for the future."

"Thank you." Frances ran a hand through her hair. "For the record, I never used drugs again."

"I'm glad to hear it." Yvonne smiled. "When your son wakes, tell him I popped by."

Frances nodded as she turned back to his bedside. "I will."

THE TEAM WAS DEBRIEFED by DCI Llewelyn the following day. "That was great teamwork, and a successful outcome for Tony Howells... Well done."

"What's happening with Peter Turner? Do we know?" Yvonne asked. "I am aware you play squash with his solicitor."

He shrugged. "I know little more than you, except a certain birdie tells me he plans to study law while he's inside."

The DI raised her brows. "Really? Wow, I wasn't expecting that."

"Strange, the way things work out... Oh, and his uncle will visit him regularly. Apparently, he feels guilty about letting Peter down when he was young. He thinks he should have spent more time with him."

"What about Peter's father?"

He shrugged. "Now that, I don't know. Our match was only a half-hour long."

She grinned. "Then, I'll let you off."

He glanced at the wall clock. "I hear La Taverna has an offer on tonight," he said, referring to the greek restaurant on Park Lane.

"I'm in!" Dai shouted, quickly followed by Callum.

Dewi cocked his head. "Are you paying, sir?"

Llewelyn laughed. "What, again?"

"We'll go halves..." Yvonne pulled a face at her team. "You guys did good."

AFTERWORD

You might also like to read the other books in the series:
    Book 1: Death Master:

After months of mental and physical therapy, Yvonne Giles, an Oxford DI, is back at work and that's just how she likes it. So when she's asked to hunt the serial killer responsible for taking apart young women, the DI jumps at the chance but hides the fact she is suffering debilitating flashbacks. She is told to work with Tasha Phillips, an in-her-face, criminal psychologist. The DI is not enamoured with the idea. Tasha has a lot to prove. Yvonne has a lot to get over. A tentative link with a 20 year-old cold case brings them closer to the truth but events then take a horrifyingly personal turn.

Book 2: You Will Die

After apprehending an Oxford Serial Killer, and almost losing her life in the process, DI Yvonne Giles has left England for a quieter life in rural Wales.Her peace is shattered when she is asked to hunt a priest-killing psychopath, who taunts the police with messages inscribed on the corpses.Yvonne requests the help of Dr. Tasha Phillips, a psychologist and friend, to aid in the hunt. But the killer is one step ahead and the ultimatum, he sets them, could leave everyone devastated.

Book 3: Total Wipeout

A whole family is wiped out with a shotgun. At first glance, it's an open-and-shut case. The dad did it, then killed himself. The deaths follow at least two similar family wipeouts – attributed to the financial crash.

So why doesn't that sit right with Detective Inspector Yvonne Giles? And why has a rape occurred in the area, in the weeks preceding each family's demise? Her seniors do not believe there are questions to answer. DI Giles must therefore risk everything, in a high-stakes investigation ofa mysterious masonic ring and players in high finance.

Can she find the answers, before the next innocent family is wiped out?

Book 4: Deep Cut

In a tiny hamlet in North Wales, a female recruit is murdered whilst on Christmas home leave. Detective Inspector Yvonne Giles is asked to cut short her own leave, to investigate. Why was the young soldier killed? And is her death related to several alleged suicides at her army base? DI Giles this it is, and that someone powerful has a dark secret they will do anything to hide.

Book 5: The Pusher

Young men are turning up dead on the banks of the River Severn. Some of them have been missing for days or even weeks. The only thing the police can be sure of, is that the men have drowned. Rumours abound that a mythical serial killer has turned his attention from the Manchester canal to the waterways of Mid-Wales. And now one of CID's own is missing. A brand new recruit with everything to live for. DI Giles must find him before it's too late.

Book 6: Gone

Children are going missing. They are not heard from again until sinister requests for cryptocurrency go viral. The public must pay or the children die. For lead detective Yvonne Giles, the case is complicated enough. And then the unthinkable happens...

Book 7: Bone Dancer

A serial killer is murdering women, threading their bones back together, and leaving them for police to find. Detective Inspector Yvonne Giles must find him before more innocent victims die. Problem is, the killer wants her and will do anything he can to get her. Unaware that she, herself, is is a target, DI Giles risks everything to catch him.

Book 8: Blood Lost

A young man comes home to find his whole family missing. Half-eaten breakfasts and blood spatter on the lounge wall are the only clues to what happened...

Book 9: Angel of Death

The peace of the Mid-Wales countryside is shattered, when a female eco-warrior is found crucified in a public wood. At first, it would appear a simple case of finding which of the woman's enemies had had her killed. But DI Yvonne Giles has no idea how bad things are going to get. As the body count rises, she will need all of her instincts, and the skills of those closest to her, to stop the murderous rampage of the Angel of Death.

Book 10: Death in the Air

Several fatal air collisions have occurred within a few months in rural Wales. According to the local Air Accidents Investigation Branch (AAIB) inspector, it's a coincidence. Clusters happen. Except, this cluster is different. DI Yvonne Giles suspects it when she hears some of the witness statements but, when an AAIB inspector is found dead under a bridge, she knows it.

Something is way off. Yvonne is determined to get to the bottom of the mystery, but exactly how far down the treacherous rabbit hole is she prepared to go?

Book 11: Death in the Mist

The morning after a viscous sea-mist covers the seaside town of Aberystwyth, a young student lies brutalised within one hundred yards of the castle ruins.

DI Yvonne Giles' reputation precedes her. Having successfully captured more serial killers than some detectives have caught colds, she is seconded to head the murder investigation team, and hunt down the young woman's killer.

What she doesn't know, is this is only the beginning...

Book 12: Death under Hypnosis

When the secretive and mysterious Sheila Winters approaches Yvonne Giles and tells her that she murdered someone thirty years before, she has the DI's immediate attention.

Things get even more strange when Sheila states:

She doesn't know who.

She doesn't know where.

She doesn't know why.

Book 13: Fatal Turn

A seasoned hiker goes missing from the Dolfor Moors after recording a social media video describing a narrow cave he intends to explore. A tragic accident? Nothing to see here, until a team of cavers disappear on a coastal potholing expedition, setting off a string of events that has DI Giles tearing her hair out. What, or who is the thread that ties this series of disappearances together?

A serial killer, thriller murder-mystery set in Wales.

Book 14: The Edinburgh Murders

A newly-retired detective from the Met is murdered in a murky alley in Edinburgh, a sinister calling card left with the body.

The dead man had been a close friend of psychologist Tasha Phillips, giving her her first gig with the Met decades before.

Tasha begs DI Yvonne Giles to aid the Scottish police in solving the case.

In unfamiliar territory, and with a ruthless killer haunting the streets, the DI plunges herself into one of the darkest, most terrifying cases of her career. Who exactly is The Poet?

Book 15: A Picture of Murder

Men are being thrown to their deaths in rural Wales.

At first glance, the murders appear unconnected until DI Giles uncovers potential links with a cold case from the turn of the Millennium.

Someone is eliminating the witnesses to a double murder.

DI Giles and her team must find the perpetrator before all the witnesses are dead.

Book 16: The Wilderness Murders

People are disappearing from remote locations.

Abandoned cars, neatly piled belongings, and bizarre last photographs, are the only clues for what happened to them.

Did they run away? Or, as DI Giles suspects, have they fallen prey to a serial killer who is taunting police with the heinous pieces of a puzzle they must solve if they are to stop the wilderness murderer.

Book 17: The Bunker Murders

A murder victim found in a shallow grave has DI Yvonne Giles and her team on the hunt for both the killer and a motive for the well-loved man's demise.

Yvonne cannot help feeling the killing is linked to a string of female disappearances stretching back nearly two decades.

Someone has all the answers, and the DI will stop at nothing to find them and get to the bottom of this perplexing mystery.

Book 18: The Garthmyl Murders

A missing brother and friends with dark secrets have DI Giles turning circles after a body is found face-down in the pond of a local landmark.

Stymied by a wall of silence and superstition, Yvonne and her team must dig deeper than ever if they are to crack this impossible case.

Who, or what, is responsible for the Garthmyl murders?

Book 19: The Signature

When a young woman is found dead inside a rubbish dumpster after a night out, police chiefs are quick to label it a tragic accident. But as more bodies surface, Detective Inspector Yvonne Giles is convinced a cold-blooded murderer is on the loose. She believes the perpetrator is devious and elusive, disabling CCTV cameras in the area, and leaving them with little to go on. With time running out, Giles and her team must race against the clock to catch the killer or killers before they strike again.

Remember to watch out for Book 20, coming later in the year

Printed in Great Britain
by Amazon

25691184R00098